A DEATH BEFORE THE WEDDING

A PINK CUPCAKE MYSTERY BOOK 10

HARPER LIN

A DEATH BEFORE THE WEDDING

ISBN: 978-1-987859-76-8

www.harperlin.com

CHAPTER ONE

THE BEAUTIFULLY AIRBRUSHED faces of over a dozen brides-to-be stared back at Amelia Harley. She had agreed to meet her best friend, Christine Mills, at the last remaining bookstore in Gary, Oregon, to chat and catch up and discuss Amelia's upcoming wedding. They'd found two comfy chairs with a coffee table in front of them where they could spread out but were still close enough to talk without disturbing anyone else. As Amelia looked at all the choices and all the price tags, she started to get cold feet.

"They all look so young and perfect," she muttered as she swept her hand across all the glossy covers.

Christine sat next to Amelia, snuggling into the

high-back armchair with her own large coffee in front of her and a magazine in her hands. "Brides can be any age. My Aunt Tootie has been married three times, and she's worn a white dress at each wedding. She even decorated her walker at the last one. It had streamers and a Just Married sign made from cardboard and glitter hanging from the front."

Amelia nearly spit out her coffee. "No she didn't." She laughed.

"I swear." Christine held up her right hand as if taking an oath. "If she can wear a wedding dress at her age, you certainly can. Stop with the false modesty. You know you're still a little hottie. Any one of these dresses would look fabulous on you."

"I don't know, Chris. Look at this one." She held up a magazine called *Exquisite Bride*. On the page was a gorgeous, rail-thin model wearing what was nothing more than the laciest, sheerest body stocking sewn with Swarovski crystals and real mother-of-pearl buttons up the back. Amelia was fairly sure wearing underpants in this number would be an impossibility.

"Okay, first, the dress is horrendous," Christine said flatly, making Amelia laugh. "Second, only a stripper would wear something like that. You and Dan aren't getting married on the Vegas Strip. You're going to have a beautiful wedding. You know what they say."

Amelia waited as Christine continued to flip through her magazines. "Well, I'm waiting. What do they say?"

"They say every bride finds the right dress for *her*. Sheesh. You'd think you've never been through this before."

"That's another thing." Amelia shook her head. "My wedding to John was a huge spectacle. It's so embarrassing now. I keep thinking, who am I to have a second wedding with all the trimmings and attention? Especially when I've got a daughter. She's going to have a special day someday and—"

"She's just turned fifteen," Christine said. "I should hope she's not making plans yet."

"You know what I mean, Chris. I don't feel like I deserve this." Amelia closed the magazine and took a sip of her coffee. She thought back to her wedding day with John. She'd been so happy, and he was so handsome, towering over her a good solid foot, his shoulders even broader in the tuxedo he wore. *Forever*, they had promised. After so many years together and two beautiful children, how could it have gone so wrong?

She remembered her big billowy dress, the

couple hundred guests, their honeymoon in Hawaii. It was beautiful, but it turned out to be nothing more than a dog and pony show. At least, that was how Amelia felt looking back on it.

"You of all people do deserve this." Christine took her friend's hand. "John was the one who cheated. John was the one who ruined everything. It wasn't you."

"I can't look at any more wedding magazines." Amelia smiled and started to arrange them in a stack. "I should be working on the second truck. That's something I can get jazzed about."

"So you're really expanding the business?" Christine asked.

"I have to. The demand is insane." Amelia smiled. "I never would have believed that my little cupcake business would have taken off like it did. I just can't believe it sometimes."

"There it is," Christine said, smiling and pointing at her friend.

"There what is?"

"That excited bride-to-be face. I think you are right. Let's put away these magazines and finish our coffee. Do you still want to go check out The Old Barn for the reception?" Christine asked before taking a sip.

"We made the appointment. We should go. I've been dying to see the place even if I weren't getting married. I've heard it's really something unique."

"Uh-oh," Christine said, looking at the door that had just been set off by a chain of jingling bells. "Don't look now, but we've got incoming missiles at nine o'clock."

Before Amelia could turn and look, she heard the high-pitched squeal of excitement. Her shoulders bunched up against the noise, and as she looked to her left, she saw Denise, Linda, and Sarah coming toward her.

"You've got to be kidding me. I don't come to the bookstore for months and the one time I do the Witches of Eastwick show up," Amelia said with an annoyed smirk on her face. It was bad enough they'd known all about John's affair for months and never breathed a word to her. But to come up to her after Amelia had made it very clear she wanted nothing to do with this nest of vipers showed even more ignorance on their part.

"Oh my gosh! I can't believe it!" Denise gushed. "What are you guys doing here?"

"Having coffee," Christine said.

"Amelia, you have no idea how much I have been thinking about you lately," Denise said.

"It's true," Sarah interrupted with a nervous smile. "She was just telling us the other day that she wondered where you've been."

That wouldn't have anything to do with my wedding announcement being in the paper about three months ago, Amelia thought but said nothing.

"She's been working," Christine offered. "In fact, we're on our way to go look at another truck. Business is booming."

"Oh, looks like you have your very own PR person," Denise jabbed.

"Amelia takes good care of her *friends*," Christine snapped back.

Amelia sensed that any minute this chance meeting might turn into a brawl. She cleared her throat and picked up *Exquisite Bride* and started flipping through the pages, falling back to the sheer dress Christine said only a stripper would wear.

"Christine and I are trying to get some wedding dress ideas," Amelia said, instantly hating she said anything. Why didn't she just let Christine tear Denise, Linda, and Sarah apart? If anyone could do it, it was Chris. Living in a house with four boys plus her husband, she was the most qualified to take down these gossipers.

"Oh, are you getting married?" Linda asked, feigning surprise.

"I told you that I read it in the paper," Sarah said, looking at Linda, who ignored her and stared at Amelia with a smile, while Denise gave Sarah a nudge with her elbow.

They hadn't changed at all from the day they told Amelia about her husband's infidelity in the middle of lunch at a full restaurant. It was not just the news that shocked Amelia, but the joy these women took in telling her about it. She couldn't say what was worse—having a cheating husband or having women who said they were her friends savoring her distress.

"Congratulations," Denise finally said. "It's about time. I mean, John moved on. It's only natural you should want to too."

"Denise, I'm getting married because I love my fiancé. Not because I feel that since John did, I should too. That's stupid." Amelia glared at Denise. "And I don't think you should comment on things you know nothing about. None of you know anything about me anymore. We travel in different circles now."

Denise swallowed hard. Linda and Sarah looked at her as if waiting for her to direct them on what to do next. She lifted her chin and quickly blinked a couple of times before clearing her throat and looking at Christine, who smiled broadly before taking a long, loud sip of her coffee.

"I thought we could bury the hatchet," Denise said.

Maybe she meant it. But that would mean she felt bad for how she and the girls had treated Amelia that day at lunch. Amelia didn't think that was their motivation. Maybe it was cynical of her, but Amelia was sure it had more to do with the Three Stooges looking for fodder and not forgiveness. They had come by the Pink Cupcake on Food Truck Alley a couple of times, but Amelia was playing the role of businesswoman and boss. She served them and was pleasant. But this wasn't the food truck, they weren't customers, and Amelia had had enough. She looked sternly at them all and said not another word.

"We just wanted to say hello and wish you luck," Linda snapped.

Amelia looked at Christine, who narrowed her eyes at the trio but kept her mouth shut.

"Fine. We'll go," Denise said before turning and stomping up to the counter to order a coffee. It reminded Amelia of high school when one clique clashed with another. Now they would get their lattes, find a table to sit at, and lean in to whisper to each other about how awful Amelia was to them.

"That was fun. Can we do some more?" Christine chuckled.

"I'm done with them for good," Amelia said, feeling a little lighter. She looked down at the wedding magazines and shook her head. "And I'm done with these. I'll just go buy something off a rack somewhere."

"You sure you don't want to look at *Novelty Bride*? Each dress comes with a boutonniere that squirts water. Oh, here we go. *Biker Bride*. No? What are you shaking your head for?" Christine asked with a straight face, making Amelia laugh even harder.

They left the bookstore, the magazines, and a good chunk of Amelia's past behind and never looked back.

CHAPTER TWO

THE OLD BARN was exactly that, a beautiful, giant red barn that was transformed into a reception hall that could accommodate an intimate party of seventy-five people or an extravagant event for up to five hundred. It was rustic and simple, yet anyone who was able to book their party there was allowed bragging rights of having celebrated their special day in the same place where the governor of Oregon's daughter had her wedding reception. Recently, the star of a comic book superhero movie also had his son's fifth birthday party there.

The property sat on top of a hill with a beautifully manicured lawn with brilliant patches of every kind of flower imaginable. Tall weeping willows added to the romance of the entire place. The long drive leading up to it was gravel until it got to the house where the owners lived. They rented out their farmhouse as a bed-and-breakfast able to accommodate about thirty guests. The wraparound porch was sprinkled with antique milk canisters, rocking chairs, and even a tub with a washboard in it. Delicate wind chimes hung from every corner of the house and were set off with the slightest breeze.

"It's like we stepped into a Jane Austen book," Christine said as they parked Amelia's old sedan at the top of the hill.

As soon as they got out of the car, a tall woman in a striking green blazer and matching skirt came hustling out of the farmhouse. She had to be about six feet tall, and that was without the stilettos she was wearing.

"Hello," she said without smiling. Her thick lips were coated with a brown lipstick, and her hair was piled on top of her head in a loose bun. "You must be Amelia Harley. We've been expecting you." The woman sniffled. Either she was coming down with a cold or she had been crying. Amelia wasn't sure.

"Yes," Amelia replied and stuck out her hand.

"I'm Sondra Hope. I'm the owner of The Old Barn. Welcome," she said, still barely cracking a smile.

Amelia went on to express how much she liked what she'd seen so far just coming up the driveway. "It's absolutely breathtaking," she said.

"Thank you. Um, if you'll excuse me for a second, I have an issue with some of the staff I must tend to. We've got a *huge* fundraiser taking place in four days and aren't nearly ready. But we will be. Why don't you walk around the grounds and look inside the old barn, and I'll be right back to answer any of your questions." Sondra looked over her shoulder as though she expected someone to come running out after her.

"Thank you. We'll do just that," Amelia said.

As soon as Sondra turned her back and headed back toward the house, Christine looked at Amelia with raised eyebrows. "What do you think that is all about?" she asked.

"I don't know. Maybe she just got some bad news, or her pet died. I couldn't even guess," Amelia replied.

"She isn't what I expected as the owner of The Old Barn. I thought it would be a chubby middle-aged farm lady wearing a flowered house dress, and her husband would be in overalls, holding a pitchfork, while she carried a basket of ripe tomatoes," Christine added.

"That's what I would have thought too. She looks like she stepped out of one of those magazines we were looking at."

Amelia nodded toward the barn. They started to walk in that direction when suddenly there was a loud shriek, the sound of something crashing, and then dead silence. From around the back of the house, a man in a navy-blue jumpsuit came rushing out. He was covered in sweat, and his eyes were wild, but he stopped as soon as he saw Amelia and Christine.

"Did you hear that?" Christine asked.

Just then, a tall man in sleek black slacks and a crisp light-gray button-down shirt came strolling out from what looked like a greenhouse attached to the house. His hands were in his pockets. His eyes shifted up, then he stopped abruptly as if he wasn't expecting to see two strangers standing near his porch.

He pulled his hands from his pockets. "What was that?" he barked while looking at Amelia and Christine.

They shrugged, and Amelia pointed toward the house. He went inside the house through the front door, letting it slam behind him. There were shuffling sounds, something glass broke on the floor, and there was grunting.

Before Amelia could say another word, the front screen door flew open, and Sondra came staggering out, her face contorted in pain, her eyes wide and yet unseeing. Her hands were held out in front of her as if she were only able to find her way by touch. After three clumsy steps, she fell over, slapping hard against the wood porch floor and revealing a pair of garden shears protruding from her back. She was dead.

"Oh my gosh!" Christine cried. "Someone call 911!"

The gardener stood there, sweating and looking around nervously, before he hurried to the work shed at the far end of the barn and disappeared inside.

Christine fumbled through her purse, muttering the entire time that she had never seen anything like it, nor had she ever wanted to. "You can't have your reception here now. There has got to be a saying from the old country warning brides not to marry where a death has occurred, or you'll be cursed with eighty years of sorrow or thick black facial hair or something equally ghoulish."

She held her cell phone up to her ear and spoke with the dispatcher, giving a quick yet gruesome account of what just happened. The thing Amelia wondered was where the guy in the sports jacket was. He was looking for Sondra just a minute ago, but now he didn't even come to the porch to see if she was all right.

Amelia ran up to her but could tell by the way her eyes stared blankly and her face was twisted in a grimace of fear that she was dead. Other than the garden tool protruding from her back, her nails, jewelry, and hair were still in place. Her right shoe had come off, exposing a perfectly pedicured foot. Amelia shook her head at Christine, who continued to speak to the dispatcher. Sirens could be heard in the distance.

"What are you doing? Get away from her!" screamed a hysterical man who looked like Superman had just stepped out of a comic book and slipped out of his superhero costume into a pair of jeans and a T-shirt and cowboy boots.

"I'm sorry. I was just trying…" Amelia stuttered before looking at Christine, who stared with her mouth open and the phone hovering away from her ear. She mouthed the word "Wow."

"He did it! I can't believe it! He finally did it! Oh, Sondra! Sondra, can you hear me?" the man blubbered like a big baby. Tears gushed from his eyes as he tried to roll Sondra over.

"You shouldn't touch her until the police arrive. You might—"

"Shut up!" he shouted. "Get away from her!"

Amelia did as she was ordered and stood next to Christine just as a slew of police cars and the ambulance arrived.

"Well, this is an ugly mess. Sir, I need you to step away from the body immediately!" shouted a plainclothes detective Amelia had never seen before. He was heavyset and waddled as he walked. "Good afternoon, ladies," he said to Amelia and Christine.

He approached the body as if he was sidling up to an all-you-can-eat buffet. Before studying Sondra, he pointed to one of the rocking chairs, and the sobbing man took a seat without issue. He continued to sob.

Within minutes, a small woman in a blue windbreaker with the word Coroner on the back came strolling up to the detective with a camera in each hand. She muttered a few words to the detective, who answered her loudly.

"Yeah. I want the video done last. Make sure to get all angles of the weapon. Her hands and feet too," the detective said. For a man of his stature, he was agile enough to get down on his hands and knees to stare directly into Sondra's dead face. After a few seconds, he grunted and pushed himself up.

"You ladies see what happened?" he asked suddenly, making them both jump.

CHAPTER THREE

DETECTIVE WALTER HOBBS was nothing like the straitlaced, just-the-facts-ma'am Detective Dan Walishovsky that Amelia had come to know and fall in love with. In fact, if Detective Hobbs was any further away on the detective spectrum, he would have been considered in an alternate universe of detecting.

"So, you say you thought she was crying when she greeted you. Do you have any idea what she might be upset about? Was she even upset? Could it have been allergies? There are tons of flowers around here. My darling Lucy wouldn't last five minutes with all this weeding. That's why we were married at the station chapel. That was over twenty-five years ago. Can you believe that? I still can't. So do you know what she might have been crying about?" He rattled everything off as if he were an auctioneer selling a tractor.

The only way Amelia and Christine knew he was done rambling was when he stopped and stared at them. His eyes were piercing little brown beads that were set back in his pudgy face. They shook their heads.

"Okay. Well, if you remember anything else, I want you to call me." Hobbs handed each of them a business card pinched between a stubby index and middle finger. His wedding ring on his left ring finger looked like it could only be removed if they either cut the gold band or amputated the finger.

"Even if it seems insignificant. The truth is, there is no such thing as an insignificant clue when it comes to murder. And I am pretty sure you ladies figured out that our victim didn't do this to herself." He scoffed. "Milly, how are my photos coming along?"

"I'm almost done with the snaps. I'll get the video started," the small woman chirped without looking up from her digital screen.

"That's a good girl," Hobbs replied. "Okay, bruiser. Can you pull yourself together enough to talk to me?"

Christine's eyes popped out of her head as she heard how Hobbs was speaking to the man sniffling in the rocking chair.

"That detective's bedside manner is horrible," Christine said.

"That's because he's not here to make people feel better. He's here to find out what happened. But he is pretty rough around the edges," Amelia replied. She had thought the same thing about Dan when she first met him. But that was before she got to know him. Once that happened, she fell in love with him. She wondered if that was what happened to Detective Hobbs and his Lucy.

"I know this probably isn't right, but I need to use the bathroom and bad," Christine said. "I never should have had that large coffee."

"Well, you didn't know the bathroom was going to be roped off behind police tape. I bet you could go in the old barn and use that one," Amelia suggested.

"Do you think there is one in there?" Christine asked.

"They couldn't very well have parties in there without them, right? People would be running back and forth to the house. Or an outhouse? There has to be a bathroom in there. Come on." Amelia led the way to the actual old barn the entire estate was named for. As they quietly slipped inside, Amelia couldn't deny the idea that having a wedding reception there would have topped her previous wedding.

There was a fireplace big enough to stand in at one end. The entire south wall was nothing but windows. Hanging from the rafters were rustic chandeliers of chicken wire, wooden wheels, and dangling mason jar lights.

There was a set of stairs to the loft above that Amelia immediately imagined her children posing on. She and Dan posing in front of the fireplace. Her guests oohing and aahing over the view. It certainly was a beautiful place.

But before she got too carried away and asked to sign on the dotted line, murder or no murder, Amelia saw someone run past the window side of the barn. It was a woman, and she was holding several files in her hands. As Amelia walked to the window to get a better look, she saw out back what looked like a smokehouse for barbecuing or drying meats.

The lady shoveled the papers into an oilcan smoker. Within seconds, a trail of smoke was curling its way up and out of the little stack at the side of the barrel. The woman stood there for a few minutes, looked around, then dashed back in the direction she'd come.

"You won't believe what's in the bathroom," Christine said, making Amelia jump and turn around with her hand to her chest. "Looks like you shouldn't have had the large coffee either."

"What's in the bathroom?" Amelia asked.

"A full-length mirror framed in antlers," Christine gushed. "I absolutely love it. I took my picture in front of it." She held up her phone for Amelia to look.

"You think something with so many pointy ends should be in your house with all the boys? Might not be a good idea," Amelia said as she linked her arm through Christine's and led her to the exit.

Christine shrugged. "So, do you think you're going to book this place?"

"What? You just said I can't because someone died here. Gruesomely, I might add. I don't think I'll ever trim my rose bushes the same way again," Amelia said as they slipped out of the barn.

"Yes, but that was before I saw the antler mirror." Christine said, walking back toward their car.

"That was the game changer for you, huh?"

"It was. It really was." Christine chuckled.

Amelia watched the uniformed police officers as they roped off the porch. The body was finally covered with a sheet and hoisted onto a gurney, which was loaded into the rear of a wagon with the word Coroner on the back, just like Milly had on the back of her jacket. Amelia suddenly realized she was referring to Sondra Hope as "it." She shook her head. That wasn't very nice. Sondra was a person, and even though Amelia had only known her for a matter of minutes, she counted. She had existed just an hour ago, and now she was no more.

The incredibly handsome and muscular man was still blubbering on the porch, nodding to the officers, who tried to talk to him after the detective had. He was pointing here and there, shaking his head, and running his hands through his hair.

"Can you believe that guy?" Christine asked as she fumbled through her purse for her keys. "I didn't know they made them that way. Do you think he works out or is it all just farm work?"

"Maybe a little of both," Amelia replied absently.

Amelia was staring in the man's direction, but he wasn't what she was looking at. She was focusing on the greenhouse and the two people inside, who looked like they were having an argument. As she squinted, Amelia was sure it was the man in the sharp slacks and the woman who had just thrown half a dozen files in the oilcan smoker.

They looked to be arguing back and forth until

something was resolved, and they both came out to talk with the police. The woman was the first to approach Detective Hobbs.

"He seems pretty broken up about what happened. Who do you think he is? Boyfriend? Husband?" Christine asked.

"I don't know. What do you say we get something to eat? I don't know about you, but I'm starved," Amelia said, making notes on the behavior of everyone, as she and Christine were given the go-ahead to leave by the police.

"You were reading my mind," Christine said.

After a nice lunch and some more chatter about the events of the day, Amelia was home just in time to beat her children getting home from school. She quickly pulled out a couple of frozen pizzas, defrosted a batch of her maple syrup cupcakes with chocolate frosting, and turned on her laptop to catch the evening news. She wondered what they'd say about the murder at The Old Barn. Turned out, they said very little.

CHAPTER FOUR

"YOU DON'T KNOW what you're talking about," Meg said to her brother as soon as they walked in the door.

"Oh, right. You're the authority on movies, considering you can't comprehend anything made after the age of color," Adam snapped back, shoving her into the doorframe in order to get in the house first.

"You just don't know good movies. You think the original *Tron* is a good movie," Meg jabbed, pushing him as he walked ahead of her.

"It's better than *Sunset Boulevard*," Adam replied, knowing that was one of his sister's favorite movies.

"Right!" she shouted. "I don't know how you exist in life."

"Can you two ever come in the house speaking nicely to each other?" Amelia asked as she walked around the kitchen table to give Adam a kiss on the forehead and get her daily kiss on the cheek from Meg.

"If Adam could keep his mouth shut for longer than a nanosecond," Meg replied simply. She bopped over to the fridge, opened it, grabbed two oranges, and tossed one to Adam.

"If Meg could ever say something that made sense," Adam replied, hoisting his backpack over his shoulder and quickly disappearing behind the basement door.

The basement had long ago been converted into Adam's bedroom-office where he tweaked and upgraded his computers in order to do all kinds of nifty things that made him happy but were lost on Amelia.

"Anything exciting happen in school today?" Amelia asked Meg before she darted upstairs to her room.

"Not really. It's a pretty slow news day. Sorry to say," she said as she started to peel her orange. "How about you? Did you have fun with Christine?"

"Oh yeah. You know we always have a good time," Amelia said.

"That's for sure. You guys could be at a crime scene and still have fun," Meg replied over her shoulder as she made her way upstairs to her room.

Amelia stood there shocked at how literally true her daughter's words were.

That night after dinner, the kids were watching the news. Amelia waited for the story about the murder at The Old Barn to run. She waited and waited until, finally, the news was over with no mention of the killing.

"Looks like it was a boring news day all over," Meg said, yawning and stretching from the couch. "Want to watch a movie with me, Mom?"

"Hey, I was going to have Amy come over to watch a movie. Her parents said she could come by while they went out on a date night," Adam said, wincing.

"Amy can come over. Meg, you can watch up in my room," Amelia said as she grabbed the laptop she was getting better and better at using and sat down at the kitchen table.

"Are you coming?" Meg asked.

"I'll be up in just a second. I need to check on something." Amelia tapped the computer keys and tried to find any local news outlets that listed the murder at The Old Barn. But there was nothing. It was like a media blackout. Sure, she knew the networks did this sort of thing to politicians. But what would be the purpose of blacking out the proprietor of one of the most successful wedding venues in Oregon being murdered? It was a mystery inside a mystery. Amelia only knew one person who might be able to help her.

"Hi," she said after getting her cell phone and dialing her favorite number.

"Well, hello, fiancée." Detective Dan Walishovsky had a deep voice that matched his tall stature and pensive expression. "What's happening?"

"Oh, nothing. Christine and I went to The Old Barn today to get a quote for a possible wedding reception."

"How did it go?" he asked.

"How did it go? Are you serious?" Amelia huffed.

"Uh-oh. Is this one of those bride things I'm supposed to be excited about? Sorry. Please tell me every detail from the floor to the ceiling to every petal on the flower arrangements to the curtains hanging over the windows. I want to know it all," he said, his voice heavy with sarcasm.

"No. That's not it." Amelia chuckled. "Do you know Detective Walter Hobbs?"

"Sure, I know Wally. He's a good guy. Why?"

"Well, I met him at The Old Barn," Amelia replied.

"What was he doing there? Planning a party for his wife, Lucy, I bet."

"No. I don't think anyone will be planning any events at this venue for some time," Amelia said.

"Why?"

Amelia went on to tell him what had happened just moments after Amelia and Christine had arrived. She also said there was no mention about any of it on the news.

"That is strange. But I know that the Hopes, who own that property, have a lot of connections in town. They might have asked for privacy at this time. Wow. You said a pair of landscaping shears? That's brutal," Dan said.

"I know." Amelia waited for a moment. "So you didn't hear anything about it at your end? No uniformed officers making comments or bringing up the horrific nature of the crime scene?"

"What are you doing, fiancée?" Dan asked suspiciously. "Please don't tell me you are thinking of getting involved in this. Do I have to remind you that you aren't a police officer or even a cadet, let alone a detective? Any snooping around could be considered evidence tampering or manipulation of a crime scene."

"Of course I'm not going to do any of those things. I'd never disturb a crime scene. I was just curious because I was there, that's all. You really need to be more trusting if we are going to be married, Detective."

"Is that so?" he asked.

Amelia could hear the slight curl on the right side of his lip that indicated he was smiling. That was the most a serious guy like Dan would display in the way of emotions. Except where Meg and Adam were concerned. He lit up like a Christmas tree when the kids came around. Especially Meg. She and Adam had been pushed aside by John when he married his new wife, who was only ten years older than Meg.

Amelia knew that Dan struggled to understand what was wrong with John and how he couldn't see the beauty in his own children. It was probably because, no matter who the kids looked like, their personalities favored Amelia. They were kind and funny and just pleasant to be around even when that person didn't deserve it, like John. Dan loved Amelia's kids as if they were his own.

"I was just asking. I saw a couple of strange things while I was there. But I'm sure Detective Hobbs is caught up with everything," she said, trying to ease Dan's mind.

"Well, if you'll give me a few hours, I'll track him down and pick his brain. See if what he knows is what you know. How does that sound?" Dan asked.

"That sounds good," Amelia replied. After a little more playful banter and a few quick *I love you*'s, they hung up. Amelia went upstairs, took a quick shower, then joined her daughter on the big bed as they watched Gregory Peck in *The Gentleman's Agreement*.

After Meg had gone to bed, Amelia found she couldn't sleep.

She crept down to the basement to find Adam still awake and talking to Amy, who had spent half the evening at their house watching television with him.

"Seriously? You guys haven't talked enough?" Amelia teased.

"Sorry, Mom. I gotta go, Amy," he said into the phone. "Yeah, I'll see you tomorrow."

"What's so important?" Amelia asked.

"Oh, nothing. We were just talking," Adam said.

The computer screen lit his face just enough for her to see his cheeks blushing. Not wanting to embarrass her son any more than she already had, Amelia quickly changed the subject.

"Hey, I can't sleep. I'm going to go pick up a few things for the truck at that grocery store that's open late. I won't be gone long. Keep an eye on your sister for me?"

"Sure, Mom. Amy and I drank the last of the chocolate milk," he confessed.

"Okay, I'll add that to the list." She tousled his hair, but the natural black curls just fell back into place. "I'll be back in about half an hour."

When she left, Amelia had every intention of going to the store. In fact, she had a fairly long list in her head that included pistachio flavoring, granulated brown sugar, and maraschino cherries, plus Adam's chocolate milk. But she had to pass by the road that led to The Old Barn, and it was too much for her not to take a quick detour.

Without knowing if there were cameras watching the property, Amelia parked her car and walked up the hill to where she and Christine had parked their car just several short hours ago. After getting to know Dan, she'd picked up a couple of tricks from him that came in very handy at times like this. One was to always keep a set of binoculars in your car as well as a flashlight. Equipped with both, she made her way onto the property.

Sneaking from tree to tree, she made her way carefully up to the house where there were still a few lights on and a police officer on duty to keep anyone from sneaking around like Amelia was doing. But she wasn't interested in going up to the house. Well, she was but not with a uniformed officer just hoping there might be some rubbernecker looking to get an eyeful of the murder scene. He'd be waiting a long time since the whole story was left off the news. Amelia only wanted to see if she could piece together what was stuffed into that oilcan smoker.

Carefully, she snuck along the perimeter of the property, staying deeply tucked into the shadows as she slipped past the house and the old barn to the smokehouse that the mysterious woman had tossed those files into. Amelia was sure she could smell the papers still smoldering even though it had been a couple hours since the whole incident took place.

After putting her hand on the drum and feeling it was only slightly still warm, Amelia carefully lifted the side of the barrel to see what was inside. With a quick look over her shoulder to make sure there was no police officer standing behind her, Amelia took her flashlight and shined it into the drum.

There was a huge pile of feathery gray ashes in the middle of the drum. Amelia poked around in it with her finger, feeling the soft texture but seeing nothing that would indicate what might have been in those files. Just as she was about to sneak back the way she came, she saw a corner of a document that the flames didn't devour. Carefully, she pulled it out and studied it closely.

The words read in part "... bequeath my tangible personal property..." The rest was burned beyond recognition. Amelia knew this was part of a will. She and John had a will drawn up shortly after Meg was born. Of course, that had been deemed null and void since his remarriage. But she knew the wording well enough to know that's what the strange woman had stuffed into the smoker. She folded the piece of paper and stuck it in her pocket before snapping off her flashlight.

"Hey, who's in there?" came the deep voice of the officer on duty.

Amelia held her breath as she looked behind her. By the light of the porch, Amelia could see the silhouette of the officer. He was in the process of pulling out his flashlight and flipping the snap off his holstered weapon. Her mouth instantly went dry as her whole body froze like a rabbit that suddenly spotted a fox.

Before she could be discovered, Amelia slowly backed away from the smoker, crouched down and, in a most unladylike maneuver, kind of crab-walked to the back of the smokehouse, staying as deep in the shadows as possible. The structure was nothing more than a three-sided shack. If the officer would just give her another couple of seconds before shining his flashlight, she could dash toward the toolshed, sneak back across the property, and run to her car.

That was her plan. It was better than nothing, and as the police officer raised his flashlight toward his shoulder, she heard him press the button to turn it on. It flashed then flickered and went out. Amelia didn't wait. She took off running toward the tool-shed. She could barely see and thought she had to look like a Keystone Cop staggering and stumbling around as fast as she could in near pitch-blackness. Suddenly, one foot sank into something soft and wet. The other followed. As she pulled herself from the muck, she knew instantly what had happened. In her haste, heading toward the outer edge of the property, she managed to find the pile of fertilizer that was probably used to cultivate the beautiful garden and plant life that surrounded The Old Barn. The smell was unmistakable.

"Oh gosh," she muttered, her face crinkling up in disgust. It seemed like the faster she tried to run to her car, the stronger the smell of fertilizer became. How could she have not seen it? How could she have not smelled it? All Amelia could think was that panic must have dulled her sense of smell while increasing her fight-or-flight response because this was an aroma that was even worse than the stench at any animal farm or even the monkey house at the zoo.

Finally, she made it to her car. Looking over her shoulder, she saw the beam of the flashlight bouncing up and down as the officer ran, sweeping the light back and forth. For a second, she thought to pull off her shoes and leave them. They were obviously ruined. But that would leave behind a clue as to her identity, and she didn't want to muddy the waters of the investigation any more than she already had.

Once inside her sedan, Amelia's eyes immediately began to water from the fertilizer smell. It overcame the inside of the car in a matter of seconds. Behind her, in the rearview mirror, she saw the police officer still looking for her. He'd know where she was as soon as she started the car, but she had to get out of there. She had to get the key in the ignition if for no other reason than to get the electric windows to go down.

She wiped her eyes with the back of her hand, gasped, coughed, and fumbled with the keys in her hand, which was shaking madly. Finally, she slipped it into the ignition, gave it a twist, and heard the engine roar to life. Without fastening her seat belt or turning on her lights, Amelia floored the gas pedal and peeled out down the road with nothing but the officer's high-beam flashlight cutting through the darkness.

With her heartbeat slowing, she fumbled along the side panel and found the button to roll down the windows. It was a cold trip to the late-night grocery store with the cool night air beating against her face, neck, and shoulders. But Amelia had to stop.

"Why didn't I go here first?" she muttered as she got out of the car. The bottoms of her pants were drenched through to her skin with the wet, smelly fertilizer. Her gym shoes had the flaky brown stuff mushed in every crevice and all over her socks. But she needed those few items from the store and didn't want to have to explain where she went to, if not the grocery store.

Even though there were only a few people scattered in the aisles, they all looked at Amelia with the same expression. They wrinkled their noses, looked her up and down, and made no effort to hide their stares.

Amelia quickly shuffled to the baking aisle, the smell of fertilizer spreading across the store. She grabbed what she needed quickly, plus a gallon jug of chocolate milk for Adam, and hurried to the self-checkout.

She quickly paid, sacked her items, and sprinted out of the store. As soon as she got back in her car, she was hit with an overpowering wave of fertilizer stench. It was in the car. How long would it take for her to get that smell out of the upholstery?

"Thank goodness I didn't drive The Pink Cupcake," she muttered as she made her way home.

CHAPTER FIVE

THE NEXT DAY, Meg and Adam both noticed the smell. Amelia had tossed her gym shoes, socks, and pants in the garbage can in the garage, but apparently there was enough of the stuff still on her bare toes to leave a trail behind her.

"I tripped over a pile of fertilizer," she admitted, leaving out where it was. "Whatever you do, don't go sit in the car. I'll need to have the inside fumigated. Here's your chocolate milk."

She slammed the jug down in front of Adam. He looked sheepish, possibly thinking that his request might have had something to do with his mother's accident.

"Dad called last night. Again," Meg said as she

pulled up a chair across from her brother and swiped the jug of milk.

"You were sleeping when I went to the store. What time did he call?" Amelia asked.

"Just a few minutes after you left," Adam said.

"He called both of you?" Once again, the mere mention of her ex-husband sent Amelia's blood pressure skyrocketing. "What did he want?"

"He wanted to talk to you. He wanted to know where you were and what was happening with the wedding," Adam admitted while shaking his head.

"Okay." Amelia bit her tongue. "I'll talk to him today. Maybe he'll quit calling you guys for nonsense."

"That's the only time he calls us," Meg said before taking a gulp of milk from the jug, her eyebrows up to the middle of her forehead.

"That's not true. Remember, your dad is a busy guy. He just doesn't know how to communicate with you. That's all. And you guys are getting older, so he doesn't know how to relate," Amelia lied.

Of course, her husband knew how to relate. His current wife was only a few years older than his son. He certainly knew how to talk to the younger generation. He just chose not to talk to his children. These days, he picked them up for their weekly visits. The kids were left babysitting John's new baby while he and Jennifer had date night. When Meg had first confessed to that being the case, Amelia was ready to march over to John's house and read him the riot act from the middle of his front yard so all the neighbors would hear. But it is a delicate balance when walking the tightrope of divorce. Anything Amelia said or did would be repeated at the courthouse, and if John could point out any reason why he shouldn't be paying child support or why his visitation should be increased, he would do it.

"It's okay, Mom. We like that little baby. She's really easygoing," Meg had said. "Besides, it's better than having to go to the places Dad likes. We have to get all dressed up in uncomfortable clothes and smile as he introduces us to people we don't know. It's boring."

So Amelia didn't rock the boat. But now that things had changed with Dan and the wedding was being planned, John had become worse than a mother hen. And it wasn't overconcern for Amelia's well-being. It never was.

"I'll call your dad," she said as she grabbed her cup of coffee and shuffled toward the stairs. "And I'll be sure to get some carpet cleaner for the smell. Unless you guys like this smell?"

"Gross, Mom!" Meg shouted.

"Meg likes it," Adam replied, earning himself a soft kick under the table.

As soon as Amelia was in her bedroom with the door closed and about to step into the shower, her cell phone rang. Speak of the devil.

"Hello, John," Amelia said with a sigh before flopping down on the edge of her bed.

"Amelia, I've been trying to get ahold of you. Don't you carry your cell phone anymore?" he snapped without so much as a "hello."

"I carry it everywhere," she said sweetly. "Maybe you were dialing the wrong number."

"Look, I need to know when you plan on talking to your lawyer about the wedding," John said. "It is imperative that you let me know when this is going to happen."

"What are you talking about?" Amelia rubbed her face. Why did it have to be like this? Why did John have to be an absolute jerk at every opportunity?

"Okay, Amelia, maybe you don't realize this, but your marriage has an impact on more than just you. I have to get things finalized at this end and that takes time and money and..."

He was taking that bullying tone with Amelia

that she'd heard for so long during their marriage and especially after their divorce. The man didn't want to stay married to her but wanted to maintain control over her. She'd decided a long time ago that that was not in the divorce settlement.

"John, I have to get ready for work. Plus, I have to go put the money down on renovating my new truck, and I don't have time to worry about you and your time and money," she said sweetly.

"New truck? What happened to the old truck?"

She could hear the hope for bad news in his voice.

"Nothing. I'm expanding. I need a new truck to meet demand," she said.

Part of her didn't want to tell him anything about her life and what was going on in it. She suffered a slight case of pride and couldn't help but lift her chin as she spoke about her business. He had, after all, pooh-poohed her idea of a baking business of her own when they were married.

"Look, Amelia, expanding a business requires more than just buying another truck. Do you have any idea what you are getting into? Do you know the responsibility? What about the kids? You are away from them enough as it is, and they need their mother to—"

"You better shut your mouth, John. Shut your mouth right now." She squeezed the phone. "Don't you dare try and tell me what my children need. I know what they need. I've always known because I'm always here. Now I have to get to work. If you need to talk to me, call Lila and schedule an appointment."

She clicked the off button and sat as tears of anger flooded her eyes. She knew she shouldn't let him get to her. But he did. He was just so condescending and rude. How could she have not seen it for so long? How could she have wanted to save her marriage to him? She swallowed hard and squared her shoulders before going into her bathroom for a quick hot shower before work.

As she let the water pull away her stress, Amelia tried to count her blessings, but, as always, John had this magical way of ruining everything. By the time she made it to Food Truck Alley, after kissing the kids goodbye and battling the early morning traffic, she was hopping mad and barely noticed the smell of fertilizer that was still lingering in her vehicle despite leaving the windows open all night. And her bookkeeper and dear friend Lila Bergman knew there was a problem immediately. Lila also knew the cause.

"Uh-oh. Let me guess. John?" Lila asked as she smoothed her hair from her face.

Amelia stomped up to the truck and hissed a good morning from between clenched teeth.

"That sounds like John, all right," Beatrice Mooch, Amelia's new baker, replied. She barely looked up, her hands and cheeks already coated with flour.

In the short time she'd been working for Amelia, Beatrice had won over her heart and taste buds with nothing more than a couple strokes of a wooden spoon and an oven continually set at three hundred fifty degrees. Beatrice was to The Pink Cupcake, what Michelangelo was to the Sistine Chapel.

"I thought once he heard about the engagement he might mellow out." Amelia slammed her purse down and flopped into one of the stools at the service window. "What was I thinking? Of course he wouldn't."

"Here." Lila handed Amelia a coffee as she took a seat across from her at the small working station they'd installed there. "What happened?"

Amelia ran through the latest drama with her ex-husband, and by the time she got it all out, she was exhausted.

"What is wrong with the man?" Amelia asked.

"Buyer's remorse," Beatrice piped up from her baking station.

"What does that even mean?" Lila asked.

"He had a perfectly good model. But something told him that he needed to upgrade, so he did," Beatrice explained.

"That makes me feel so much better. John upgraded from me." Amelia pouted out her lips, her eyelids lazy over her eyes.

"But, once he has the new model, he realizes it's more work, more money, more worry and starts to remember that there wasn't all that much wrong with his original model." Beatrice's hands flew in all directions as she added spices and colorings and sprinkles and everything within arms reach into the batter. "I could be wrong but I don't think I am. Especially since the stock for his original model went up the minute she left him. Meanwhile, his new model was worth less the second he took her off the lot."

"You are a regular poet, Beatrice." Amelia smiled. "Being compared to an automobile never made me feel so good."

"She's right," Lila added. "He can't stand that you've survived without him and took back all the control he was used to having. The man just doesn't cope well."

"I didn't want to do this, but I think, as soon as the wedding is over, I'm going to hand off all dealings with John to Dan. I think it will be a lot better doing that. Not that John will be nicer to Dan. He probably won't be. But at least he'll have to show a level of respect. Dan isn't afraid of telling the highway patrol to keep a look out for John's BMW. John might find himself in even more debt as the speeding tickets just keep racking up."

"Speaking of the wedding, how did your visit to The Old Barn go? Did you book it?" Lila asked. Obviously, she hadn't heard anything about the murder either.

"Well, let me tell you."

She explained the whole gory story to the girls and wrapped it up just as they opened for business. She didn't tell them about paying a late-night visit to the crime scene, however. But that reminded her of the torn piece of paper she had absconded with. A tiny piece of a will. What could it mean? Maybe that strange woman who ran out to the smokehouse was just getting rid of some outdated paperwork. Maybe that was policy to burn old documents and prevent any kind of fraud. Or maybe she was trying to destroy something that would impact the business should it fall into the wrong hands.

Amelia mulled it over and over in her head as she and the girls opened to a line of customers waiting for the daily special, PB&J cupcakes, and cornbread cupcakes with maple bacon.

The day zoomed by and was busier than usual. The blue sky had white clouds roll past, covering the sun, and the only break Amelia was able to take was five minutes when Dan called and asked if she and the kids would like to go out for dinner.

"Adam is going to the skateboard shop with a couple of friends, and Meg is going to go home with Katherine. I guess you are just stuck with me," Amelia said, letting out a huge sigh.

"Oh, that will be terribly awkward," Dan replied, telling her to wear something nice and that he'd pick her up at six thirty.

When Amelia got off the phone, Lila had another comment to make.

"I swear you are easier to read than a Dick and Jane book," Lila teased. "What did Dan have to say?"

"We're going for dinner together. The kids have plans, so it will be just the two of us. To tell the truth, it hasn't been just Dan and I for a long while. He's so great with the kids. I mean, he really cares about them, and they like him too."

"You're lucky," Lila said as she took the money from the till and started counting. Once again, it was almost too much to fit in the bank bag. After she finished running the numbers and balancing the register, she handed Amelia the bag for the deposit.

"Well, I guess now is as good a time as any. You guys know that the second truck will be ready soon," Amelia said. Lila and Beatrice both nodded. "Well, Beatrice, you are going to be calling the shots on one truck. Lila and I decided that was best. Now, we need to hire another baker. I'm still going to be involved with the day-to-day operations, but my time will be split between the two trucks. So do you have any suggestions as to who might want to work for us?"

Lila and Amelia looked at Beatrice. The petite woman slowly took a seat, folded her hands in front of her, and looked off into the distance.

"I know a person," she said seriously.

Amelia was waiting for her to launch into a story about the USS Indianapolis delivering the bomb during World War II and how Beatrice would never wear a life jacket again. Her face grew grave and her eyes sharp.

"What's her name?" Lila asked carefully, seeming to sense Beatrice's tension.

"Him. Lionel Hascolm," Beatrice said cryptically.

"Is there something wrong with him?" Amelia asked.

"Only if you think having the ability to create decadent pastries with his eyes closed and one hand tied behind his back is wrong. He was my nemesis in baking school." Beatrice lifted her chin.

"Well, I wouldn't want you to have to work alongside someone who made you uncomfortable," Amelia said only to be cut down by Beatrice's intense stare.

"Uncomfortable? More like awe-inspiring. He was the master, and I the lowly student. As much as I tried to keep up, he bested me at every turn. And now, look at this. I am looking to have my own creations measured up to his again." She slowly stood from her seat, her chest out, and her head back.

"Beatrice, I just need someone who can bake." Amelia started to giggle as Lila poked her in the side.

"No. You've come too far. The Pink Cupcake has come too far to just settle for a baker. You deserve the best. The Pink Cupcake does. But let me ask you this." Beatrice looked at Lila and Amelia as if she were about to warn them they might have to wear garlic around their necks, carry crucifixes with them, and, on occasion, pound a stake in someone's heart. "Are you ready for your business to explode off the chart? Because, if Lionel Hascolm becomes your next baker, that is exactly what is going to happen."

Amelia looked at Lila and then back at Beatrice. "Rock and roll, Beatrice," was all she said.

"Excellent." Beatrice smirked while rubbing her hands together.

For another ten minutes, the ladies bustled around The Pink Cupcake, getting everything ready for the following day. Beatrice left quickly, her short legs moving at breakneck speed. She promised to talk to Lionel this very evening.

"That girl is as weird as they come. I just love her. You never know what to expect," Lila said as she and Amelia waved to Beatrice as she sped past in her smart car.

"Are you kidding? I can't wait to get a load of Lionel Hascolm. If he's bested Beatrice at every turn, we may as well start planning our retirement." Amelia chuckled.

CHAPTER SIX

AMELIA HAD PUT on a simple black skirt with a white sweater and black heels for her dinner with Dan. He showed up right on time and still, even though they were engaged, rang the doorbell. He had a key but refused to use it until they'd said their vows, and everything was official.

"What kind of example would it be for the kids if I just came and went? It looks bad," he said one afternoon when he'd come by after working late.

Amelia had kissed him after that comment and told him that after a nap she'd make him a bacon, lettuce, and tomato sandwich with extra bacon.

When she opened the door, he looked her up and down and let out a whistle. "I almost forgot what you looked like without two teenagers attached to either side of you."

"Funny," she said as she locked up the house. "Where are we going?"

"I thought, since it was just you and me, that maybe we'd try something new. There's a place I heard a lot of nice things about not far from the station. They've got a piano player and low lights and drinks with little umbrellas in them. What do you say?" Dan offered her his arm as they strolled to his old sedan.

"I think that sounds great. They do have food there too?" she teased.

"Steak. Ribs. Pork chops," Dan replied.

"That sounds great." She squeezed his strong arm before climbing into the passenger seat of the car. Within seconds, they were on their way.

The restaurant's name was Humphrey's. Inside, there was a framed picture of Humphrey Bogart in his white coat and black tie from his most famous movie, *Casablanca*. There were quite a few people waiting for a table, and the entire bar was full.

"Looks like we might have to go somewhere else," Amelia muttered.

"Give me a minute," Dan said then kissed her on the top of her head before making his way through the people to talk with the hostess. The young girl with arms like Olive Oyl winked at Dan before nodding her head and holding up her index finger. He smiled as much as Dan ever smiled, which was nothing more than the right side of his lips curling up slightly. Amelia noticed the men in their fine pressed suits looking suspiciously at Dan in his much cheaper and wrinkled suit as he skirted past them.

"What did you do? Slip her a tip?" Amelia asked.

"Her dad is a cop. I've known him for years," Dan whispered.

"Well done, Detective." Amelia smiled just as the hostess waved them over and took them to their table.

The evening was going pleasantly. Dan and Amelia had both ordered a glass of wine, a calamari appetizer, and a couple of steaks with all the trimmings when movement out of the corner of the room caught Amelia's eye. And Amelia wasn't the only one. All eyes were on the blonde in the purple dress, who slinked from her table to the ladies' room.

"Did you see that woman?" Amelia asked.

"She was pretty hard to miss," Dan admitted.

"I didn't know Gary had women like that in it. You ever seen her before?" Amelia's eyebrows were up.

"You mean, did I ever bust her for taking money for companionship?" Dan asked. "No. I'd have remembered."

"Is that really what she is? Maybe she is just carefree. If you've got it, flaunt it. I know if I had all that at her age, I'd flaunt it." Amelia chuckled. "I think the wine is getting to me."

"You think?"

"Who is she with? What table did she come from?" Amelia casually stretched her neck and looked around. Within a few minutes, the blonde came back and took her seat at a small intimate table for two. The man sitting across from her was an all-too-familiar face. Amelia's mouth fell open.

"Is something the matter?" Dan asked.

"I can't believe I almost forgot to ask you about this." Amelia leaned forward to whisper over the spray of flowers and the tealight candle in the middle of the table. "John called me this morning, and it literally pushed everything else out of my mind."

"John called? What about?" Dan's shoulders squared, and his blue eyes glinted.

"Never mind that now. That man over there was at The Old Barn yesterday," Amelia whispered.

"So?"

"He was in the house when Sondra Hope came

staggering out onto the porch," she said. "And now he's here, having a fancy, expensive dinner with a woman who looks like *Tomcat Magazine*'s Miss February. That's a little suspicious, don't you think?"

"Maybe," Dan said. "But let's not go jumping to conclusions. Maybe that's his sister or a business associate or—"

"Still. He was at The Old Barn when the owner stumbled out with garden shears sticking out of her back," Amelia hissed. "How can he eat after seeing that?"

"You're eating," Dan replied.

"That's different." Amelia huffed and crossed her arms over her chest. Still, her eyes were drawn to the man and the blonde.

"Look, let's just have a nice dinner, and if it will make you feel any better, I'll pass this little nugget of information along to Hobbs," Dan said. "Will that make you happy?"

Amelia nodded, but her eyes kept going back to the couple at the dark and intimate table. When the food arrived, Amelia realized she was famished. She and Dan talked about the wedding, and she explained what John had wanted when he called, all the while enjoying perfectly broiled steaks with baked potatoes. It was perfect timing when Dan decided to use the men's room that the man from The Old Barn stood up with his coat check ticket in his hand.

Amelia made her move. She followed him for a few steps before tapping him on the shoulder.

"Can I help you?" he asked.

"I see you're feeling better," Amelia said.

"I beg your pardon?"

"Since yesterday. I see you are feeling better." She put her hands on her hips.

He scoffed at her. "Do I know you?"

"Not really. I was at The Old Barn yesterday," Amelia said. "I saw you come out of the greenhouse and then go into the main house just seconds before Sondra Hope came stumbling out with a pair of garden shears sticking out of her back. But I'm glad to see it hasn't affected your appetite or anything else." She jerked her chin in the direction of the blonde.

The man grabbed Amelia by the arm and pulled her away from the crowded bar and the coat check closet a few steps down from the kitchen. "Who are you?"

"Amelia Harley."

"Are you a cop?" he asked.

"No. But I know a thing or two about—"

"Then I don't need to explain myself to you." He sneered. "But for the record, I didn't touch Sondra. In fact, when I went into the house, I didn't even see her. Even if I had, she wouldn't let me touch her. She hadn't let me touch her in over four years. Why should the fact she was dying change that?" he said bitterly.

Amelia stared.

"I'm her husband. Samuel Hope." He stared at Amelia, but it was obvious from his expression that he was seeing his past. "We were married for ten years. In the first six years, we opened The Old Barn. In the last four years, she hired and fired over a dozen lovers and gave me no explanation, no reason for her looking for love outside our marriage."

"Mr. Hope, you have to admit it looks strange you're here so soon after the tragedy, with a woman like that..." Amelia pointed to the intimate table for two.

"What are you talking about? I've been out with Bonnie a dozen times. And when I'm not with her, I'm with Tiffany or Crystal. What does it matter? Sondra left me no choice but to seek comfort elsewhere. She knew what I was doing, and I knew what *she* was doing," Samuel said through clenched teeth.

"So now you have the business and the women and—"

"Look, Amelia Harley. I wouldn't go spouting off about things I know nothing about. And I'd suggest you butt out of my affairs." He scowled.

"Interesting choice of words," Amelia snapped back before watching Samuel stomp back to his table and order Bonnie to quickly leave with him. Amelia went back to her table and waited for Dan. But before he returned, Samuel stomped up to her table.

"If you are really interested in finding out who killed my wife, I'd suggest you check with her assistant, Malcolm Wayne. I know you saw him. You can't miss him. Muscular guy. Rocks for brains. At least, that's the act he puts on. He'll be at the Wedding Expo downtown all weekend, holed up in the best suite in the entire hotel on her credit card, I'm sure." Then he turned on his heel and left.

Amelia remembered the man Samuel was talking about. He was hard to forget and not just because of the way he looked but because of the way he was acting. Maybe if Samuel would have acted a little more like the assistant, Sondra wouldn't have looked elsewhere.

She found herself having a hard time swallowing Samuel's story about Sondra icing him out. She could just as easily hear those words coming from John's mouth when he was courting Jennifer. Hell, he said something similar when Amelia caught him with someone who wasn't Jennifer. *He* was the victim. *He* was the one being used and taken for granted. Amelia didn't buy it. But she wasn't going to ignore his tip and thought a trip to the Wedding Expo was just the ticket.

"Did you get all your information?" Dan asked as he took his seat across from Amelia, smoothing his tie in the process.

"What?"

"Are you really going to try and tell me you didn't talk to that guy?" His eyes twinkled.

Amelia smiled as her cheeks flared with embarrassment. "I did. You got me." She put her hands up and shook her head.

"So tell me what he said, and I'll pass it all along to Hobbs. You can back off now. Don't you have a wedding to plan and a new truck to work on?" Dan asked, taking her hands across the table.

"Yeah, I do have those things floating out there," she replied.

As she relayed the story Samuel had told her, she watched Dan's reaction. She was happy to hear he thought the same thing she did. The *poor me* routine just didn't fly. And there were only so many reasons for one person to kill another.

"Most of the time it is either sex or money," Dan said. "Sounds like in this case, it could go either way or be both."

"He has a lot to gain. The Old Barn is a cash cow," Amelia added. "It was really beautiful. Wide open spaces and Christine fell in love with this mirror in the bathroom that was framed in antlers."

"I don't think pointy things and Christine's brood are a good mix." Dan smirked.

"That's exactly what I said." Amelia chuckled.

CHAPTER SEVEN

THE TREASURABLE MOMENTS Wedding Expo was the Disney World for brides-to-be, their mothers and mothers-in-law, maids of honor and bridesmaids, all the way down to flower girls, ring bearers, and even those who have their pets involved in the "Big Day."

The Gary, Oregon, Convention Center's main exhibit area was gigantic and arranged in rows divided into several categories. Of course, half the place was dedicated to wedding dresses. The bridesmaids and groomsmen were in a subcategory. Accessories were in a subcategory of that. Seamstresses showcased their finest alterations and transformations. Destination wedding and honeymoon planners were available to talk to. There were also photographers who boasted traditional wedding photography of brides in their white gowns and grooms in their tuxedoes, or who specialized in theme weddings, featuring photos of a wizard and sorceress tying the knot as well as a man and woman on their motorcycles with leather jackets and biker boots.

Amelia had attended the Restauranteur and Food Truck Expo before she had started The Pink Cupcake and had a great time talking with people and sampling their specialties. This was a whole other ball game, and she suddenly hoped her beautiful daughter would elope when she met her Prince Charming.

Along the back wall of the auditorium was where the organizers of the event had positioned all of the reception venues that every young bride would love to rent. There was a booth for Sebastian Castle, a huge facility that hosted not just weddings but fundraisers and charity events and thrilled the attendees by having them cross a moat to enter and boasted a taste of the Renaissance with every modern luxury.

Amelia also strolled pasts booths promoting traditional banquet halls, one-stop shops where you could get married, have dinner, and the reception all in the same place. The VFW had a small table that was packed with ladies, who were all saying, "*I never even thought of this!*" as they looked at the simple brochures that showed lovely rooms, big dance floors, and reasonable prices.

"You're getting a lot of foot traffic," Amelia said to the plump older lady at the VFW booth, who was wearing an American flag pin on her red blouse.

"We always do. The hall will be booked for almost the entire year after this show." She winked. "People don't always know what's possible until you show it to them."

"That's true." Amelia smiled and gave the woman a business card. "Maybe we could do some business together."

"Do you make patriotic cupcakes?" the lady asked.

"I can," Amelia said proudly.

"I'll be in touch." The woman raised Amelia's card before stuffing it in her pocket.

If a little business could be drummed up, maybe this wouldn't be a complete waste of time, Amelia thought. As she was nearing the end of the row, she finally spotted a booth for The Old Barn. How she could have possibly missed it was a mystery since it was like a miniature barn with balloons and props of hay and corn stalks.

Malcolm Wayne, the man who had grabbed Sondra Hope's lifeless body was there and, much like Mr. Samuel Hope, didn't seem to be all that bothered by the fact he held his boss's dead body in his arms while blubbering inconsolably just two days prior.

He was a feast for the female eyes, though, Amelia had to admit. He was over six feet tall, and his shoulders were so broad he could probably carry a piano on his back without a problem. He was wearing expensive-looking slacks, a button-down shirt opened at the collar to reveal a single gold chain, and a thick, clunky wristwatch. He spoke softly but intently as he looked deeply into the eyes of every woman who had any question to ask him, making them feel like they were the only person in the room. The young brides fell for it hook, line, and sinker, Amelia could tell. Quite a few of the mothers also asked unnecessary questions in order to lean a little closer and inhale what Amelia imagined was very expensive cologne.

There was no way Amelia was going to be able to talk to him with all these women interrupting and tripping over themselves to chat with him. The idea of staying at this event until closing time made her heart sink. Even though she was a bride-to-be herself, none of this stuff made her feel giddy about her upcoming special day.

As much as she tried to get interested in the dresses and the flowers and all that stuff, she just couldn't. She looked down at the beautiful ring Dan had proposed to her with and smiled. That was all she wanted. Simple and easy and none of this big ballooning, expensive stuff. Once she decided that, she looked back at the display for The Old Barn and saw Malcolm passing the torch on to a lovely young lady Amelia hadn't seen on the day of the murder. Before he could get lost in the crowd, Amelia followed Malcolm.

He strutted like a prize peacock through the event. More than once, he looked over his shoulder to follow the gaze of a young woman who had passed him by. The guy was a hound. There wasn't anything in a skirt over the age of eighteen and under the age of eighty that he didn't check out. Amelia was sure that he had a list of very short criteria in his head that he held each woman to as they walked by. They had to be female. They had to have breasts. And everything else was ornamental.

The convention center was attached to the Merryman Hotel by a long walkway that stretched over the main thoroughfare. Amelia walked a few paces behind Malcolm and followed him up the escalators, through an atrium, and finally down the walkway that lead to the hotel lobby.

"Good afternoon, Mr. Wayne," a pretty girl at the concierge desk said as Malcolm walked by.

"Hello, Amy," Malcolm replied, giving her a lingering look before heading toward the elevator bank.

Amelia followed him and quickly opened her purse, tucked her chin down, and pretended to be searching for her key as she stepped into the elevator.

"Oh, where is it?" She huffed. "I know it's in here."

"Lose your key?" Malcolm asked, giving Amelia his most innocent smile.

"Why are they so easy to lose? I remember putting it in here." She huffed then sighed and smiled back. Without hesitating, Malcolm swiped his card against the sensor under the row of buttons and pressed the nine for his floor.

"May I?" Amelia asked.

"Of course." Malcolm swooped his arm across the panel of numbers. "Take your pick."

"I'm on ten. Thank you," she said, closing her purse.

"Are you here for the convention?" he asked pleasantly.

"Oh, you mean all that wedding stuff? No. I'm just staying here for a little R and R," she lied. "Just looking to relieve some stress and have a good time. Leave the real world outside the door, you know?"

She felt sleazy and gross uttering these words, but Malcolm didn't seem to notice. He smiled broadly and nodded. He really was good-looking, but there was a microscopic layer of sleaze on him that made Amelia's insides recoil.

"I know exactly. My name is Malcolm," he said as the elevator pinged, and the doors slid open on the ninth floor. "I'm in suite 909. In case you are looking for a place to have a good time."

He stepped off the elevator and looked over his shoulder briefly before heading down the hallway. Amelia couldn't believe her ears. Did these kinds of lines really work on women? Were these the kinds of lines Sondra Hope fell for? Amelia had to admit that she didn't know who was worse: Samuel Hope or Malcolm Wayne. But before she had a chance to talk herself out of it, she stopped the doors from closing, peeked her head out, and called to Malcolm.

"Would you have a little time to talk?" She batted her eyelashes.

The smile on Malcolm's handsome face was the same face Amelia had seen her son Adam make when she told him he could have a second slice of chocolate cake on his third birthday. This guy was nothing but a little boy in an oversized, finely chiseled body.

"But of course," he said, swiping his card past the panel over the doorknob and holding the door open for Amelia.

Her heart was pounding as she walked up to him, adjusting the strap of her purse over her shoulder as she slinked into his room, praying no one saw this and got the wrong idea. It was bad enough that Malcolm had the wrong idea. As soon as she walked in, she remembered the words Samuel had said about having the finest suite at the hotel on Sondra's dime.

The place was huge, with a dining room, a sitting area, a kitchenette, and she knew at both ends were the bedrooms. She was going nowhere near those.

"Can I get you something to drink? I know the bar is fully stocked," Malcolm said as he shuffled over to the mini fridge in the kitchenette.

"No. Actually, I feel I have to come clean. I've seen you before," Amelia said.

"Oh, really?" He smirked as if this was some kind of game to him. "Where?"

"At The Old Barn." She cleared her throat. "Two days ago. When Sondra Hope fell onto the porch with those... uh... shears sticking out of her back." She jerked her thumb over her shoulder then smirked at Malcolm. "That was a pretty dramatic performance you put on, holding onto her, crying and sobbing, carrying on."

"Who are you?" Suddenly, he looked embarrassed and shocked.

"Amelia Harley," she replied, her heart beating a mile a minute. "You were in the house with her. What could she have possibly done to make you so mad? Gardening shears?"

"What? I only heard her stagger out of the house. You can't prove I did anything. I loved her. I would have done anything for her. We were a team. I'm devastated that she's gone." Malcolm sniffled, but there were no tears.

"That's not what I heard." Amelia wrinkled her nose. "Samuel Hope had quite a different take on it."

"Oh, right. I should have known Sam put you up to this. He was just jealous." Malcolm huffed before starting to pace back and forth.

"What would her *husband* have to be jealous

of?" Amelia asked. "Let me guess. You had bigger biceps than him?"

"Very funny. I work hard to look the way I do. I don't think I want to talk to you anymore," Malcolm said, running his hand through his hair before stomping to the door like a boy who was just told "no" for the first time.

"Who is paying for this lovely suite?" Amelia asked. "No one knows about the murder yet, isn't that right? It's been kept from the press because of family connections. That probably means no one in the hotel would ask any questions about Sondra Hope's credit card being used after she was already dead."

Malcolm stopped, his head fell forward, and those big, broad shoulders folded inward.

"What do you want? Money? Because I don't have anything." He straightened stiffly and stared.

Amelia cringed. "No. Of course I don't want any money."

"I don't have any money. This watch is a fake. I bought it from a guy in Chinatown," Malcolm babbled. "And these shoes are from a thrift store in Lake County. I won't shop anywhere around here or someone might recognize me and think I'm cheap."

"There's nothing wrong with being frugal," Amelia muttered.

"And Sondra said I could use her credit card. She said whatever I needed, I could get. She didn't say that it was only for work-related items. She should have said that if that was what she meant." Malcolm continued to rattle off his sins. "Besides, she was getting what she wanted from me. And I wasn't the only one. So if anything, I'm the real victim here."

"Malcolm, the woman is dead. Murdered. Do you want to explain to me how you are the victim?" Amelia almost laughed, but the fact Malcolm saw himself this way was too infuriating. Not to mention how disappointing that behind all that muscle and thick hair was a whiny, spoiled little boy.

"Well, I have to live with this. With that horrible memory." Once again, he pretended to wipe a tear from his eye. "You see, Sondra and I, well, we were having a relationship."

There it was. Amelia narrowed her eyes and listened as Malcolm made every attempt to make their affair understandable, if not acceptable. He was talking to the wrong woman.

"Sam was jealous of her. It's as simple as that. She made The Old Barn a success. He came along for the ride. And, in order to make her feel bad about herself, he flaunted all his girlfriends right in front of her. What would you expect her to do? Just sit back and take it?" Malcolm looked at Amelia for an answer. When she said nothing, he rolled his eyes. "Of course she wasn't going to. She was going to beat him at his own game. So she hired me." He tried to act confident again, but Amelia had already seen him fake cry, so any effort to look tough was useless.

"Now, I heard that Samuel still had feelings for her but that she wouldn't reciprocate. That it was Sondra who flaunted her lovers around the place. And apparently, she had more than one."

This news seemed to knock Malcolm off-balance. He looked to the side and then down at the floor as if he knew it were true but was trying to keep his alpha position.

"Malcolm, do you have any idea who would have done that to Sondra? You were the only one in the house," Amelia said.

"I get it. You're another one of those private investigators that Sam hired. Well, I have nothing to hide. And I'm not saying another word and you can't make me." He folded his arms like a spoiled child and harrumphed. Amelia nodded and adjusted her purse strap over her shoulder before heading toward the door.

"And I wasn't the only one in the house. Rosa was there, snooping and lurking around like a spider," Malcolm hissed.

"Who is Rosa?"

"Rosa the snitch. She always pretended to be on Sondra's side. But I could tell by the way she looked around that she was out for herself. Her and Ronny."

"Who's Ronny?" Amelia was starting to get dizzy.

"Ronny? He's the gardener. Those were his shears sticking out of Sondra's back. Poor Sondra." He sniffled.

"Oh, save it already," Amelia snapped and stomped toward the door. She pushed Malcolm to the side and stormed out into the hallway, letting the door fall shut behind her with a clang and a click.

This was starting to sound like the script of some bad afternoon soap opera. The husband of the successful businesswoman is cheating, the successful businesswoman is also cheating, now the lover of the murdered wife is implicating the maid and the gardener? The only things missing were someone getting pregnant, someone else ending up in the hospital from a suspicious car accident, and a huge cocktail party where all the suspects would be in one room, nervously waiting to be exposed by the police chief, who just happens to show up.

When Amelia got back to the convention center, she thought she was drunk. "Never judge a book by its cover," she muttered as she pushed her way through the sea of brides-to-be. Looking at wedding plans was the last thing she wanted to do.

"I love Dan," she said to Christine over the phone as she walked to her car. "But I just can't see myself putting together another scene like I did with John. It was bad luck the first time. I want things to be different with Dan."

"You don't think the fact that you may have just spent twenty minutes alone in a room with a murderer has anything to do with feeling stressed?" Christine asked, making Amelia laugh.

"Maybe you're right."

"Of course, I am." Christine laughed right back. "Look, I'll stop by the house and make sure the kids are fed, and no one is setting any fires or getting arrested. Why don't you go do something *you* like? Just for yourself. A little pampering never hurt anyone. But going without pampering has been known to cause psychosis. If I hear either one of you say '*shut up*' again, you are both going to get soap in your mouths! Don't '*but Mom*' me!"

"You are the best, Chris." Amelia laughed.

"I'm glad someone knows it." Christine chuckled before hanging up.

Normally, Amelia would take a suggestion like Christine's and tuck it way in the back part of her mind and return to fretting about whatever it was she was fretting about. But this time was different. She decided to not only take her advice but take it as far as she could.

CHAPTER EIGHT

"WHERE HAVE YOU BEEN?" Meg asked as soon as Amelia walked in the door.

"Why? What's wrong?" Amelia asked, hurrying up to her daughter, who was standing in the kitchen, nervously wringing a dish towel. "Where's Adam? Where's Christine?"

"Adam is downstairs. Christine is in the bathroom. Dad's been calling. He said he's on his way over," Meg said.

"What for?" Amelia tried to control her voice. It wasn't Meg she was mad at. But she couldn't imagine what kind of bee had gotten into John's bonnet now.

"He didn't say. He just kept asking for you and wanting to know where you were and what you were doing. I started to cry because it sounded like something was wrong, and then Christine took the phone and—"

"Oh Lord," Amelia muttered. "I can only imagine what she said."

Meg's eyes widened as she nodded. "She took the phone upstairs, but Adam and I heard her. I don't think being quiet is in her nature."

"What did she say?" Amelia asked, leaning back as if Meg's words might reach out and slap her.

"I'll tell you exactly what I said," Christine replied as she came from upstairs. "I told him if he'd paid as much attention to you and the kids when you all were married, he wouldn't be in the position he was in now. Then I told him he could go take a long walk off a short pier. That's when he said he was coming over."

"Anything else?" Amelia asked.

"No. Look, Amelia, I just can't pretend to like the guy. I just can't." Christine looked at Meg. "The only thing he did right was make these beautiful kids of yours. I'm sorry, honey. I shouldn't have said those things to your dad."

"Yes, you should have." Meg started to cry. "It's true. He doesn't care about us unless he wants something."

"I don't think that's true, honey," Amelia said. "He loves you. He just doesn't know how to communicate with you guys anymore. I think he's got problems at home, and he's taking them out on—"

Just then, there was a knock on the door. Christine told Meg to go to her room as Amelia went to the door. But before she could get up the stairs, Amelia had opened the door.

Dan was standing there.

"Oh, it's you." Amelia sighed with relief.

"I hope that's okay," he said as he stepped inside. As soon as he saw Meg, he asked, "Meg, everything okay?"

"I..." She nodded her head as if she was trying to say yes, but before Amelia could go to her, she'd dashed down the stairs and into Dan's arms, sobbing.

"What happened?" he asked, his blue eyes full of concern.

"John called. I guess he's on his way over and..." Amelia shook her head. She was embarrassed for the kids and for herself. What was wrong with the man she'd spent half her life with? He remarried. He had a new baby to tend to. He had his business and his clients and his work to deal with. Where on earth did he get the time and energy to cause so much chaos in their lives?

"He's on his way over now?" Dan asked as he stroked Meg's head.

Amelia had seen the look in his eyes before. They hardened like blue diamonds and glistened with a coldness that was reserved for hardened criminals and John.

"I guess so. That's what the kids said." Amelia sighed. "Christine, I think you should go home. It's all right."

"Are you sure? Because you might need a witness or something?" Christine asked.

"No, it's okay," Amelia said as she opened the front door.

Christine nodded and kissed Meg on the back of the head before giving Amelia a kiss on the cheek. She patted Dan on the shoulder as she slipped out the front door. Amelia watched her pull out of the driveway and drive off before she shut the door. Dan had led Meg to the kitchen and asked her to tell him everything her dad had said. When she repeated it, it sounded ridiculous.

"So, he's on his way over because your mom wasn't here?" Dan asked Meg as he wiped her tears away.

"That's what he said." She sniffled.

Just then, Adam came up from the basement.

"Dan, you've got to get our dad to stop." Adam hadn't been crying. But it was obvious from the look on his face that he'd been affected by this latest stunt. It was nothing new. John had been doing this for a while. But something had changed in the kids. Maybe they'd grown up a little more than Amelia had realized. Maybe they were just as tired of the drama as she was. Maybe they realized they didn't deserve this kind of treatment from anyone, especially their father.

Dan looked at Adam. Without smiling or winking or anything, he just nodded. Just then, there was a pounding on the front door. Everyone but Dan jumped.

"Adam. Meg. Go to your rooms," Amelia ordered. Both her children did as they were told before Amelia looked at Dan. He got up from the kitchen table and calmly strolled to the door. Again, John pounded.

"Meg! Adam! It's your father! Open the door!"

Dan yanked the door open. "What is it that's so important, John, that you need to come pounding on the door, scaring the kids and Amelia half to death?" Dan asked through clenched teeth.

It was obvious from John's body language that he hadn't expected to see Dan. He must have thought his car was Christine's and was ready to throw his weight around. That plan had come to a quick end.

"The kids were home alone. Again. Amelia is never here, and our children are left to fend for themselves. It's a disgrace," John sputtered.

"The legal age for a child to be left home alone in Gary, Oregon, is twelve, John. Were you aware of that?" Dan asked as he stepped out onto the porch, forcing John to step back. "Are you aware your children are well over that age? Are you aware that your children, regardless of your intrusions and manipulations, are two of the sweetest and most responsible children I've ever seen in my years in law enforcement?"

"Look, this is between Amelia and me. Those kids are ours and—"

"Not for much longer, they aren't." Dan took another step, forcing John off the porch. "You know, John, you have a way of ruining things for Amelia and the kids, but now it's spreading. I'm sure your wife and new baby could use your help, but you're too busy trying to bully people here. I'm sure there is some big-time client paying you a couple hundred an hour, thinking you are doing everything to help their lawsuit, and instead you are here. Well, I'm going to put an end to all of it."

"What are you going to do? Arrest me? You can't. Those kids are mine. I have a right to see them," John spat.

"You will, but I'll be a real father to them. I would adopt them if I could." Dan cleared his throat, put his hands on his hips, and Amelia was sure it was no accident that the weapon under his arm peeked out from his jacket. "You see, I love those kids. And I'll do anything for them. That includes protecting them from anything that I think might cause them harm. Even if it's you."

John looked as if he'd been punched in the stomach. Amelia wasn't even sure she'd heard Dan correctly. She stood in the doorway, thinking she'd had too long of a day or maybe drifted off into a daydream right there. But, as Dan continued to talk John backward, toward his BMW, the words were unmistakable.

"John, you've done the best you can. You can let go now. And if you think that you can stop me with any threats of legal red tape, I'm just going to remind you that not only do I know just about every judge in this county, but I also know of some private investigators, who would love to sink their teeth into a fancy, high-profile lawyer like yourself and see what they can dig up." Dan walked over to the SUV, pulled the driver's side door open and stepped out of the way. "Anytime the kids want to see you, they'll let you know. And by God, you better drop everything to accommodate."

"You can't offer them anything. They'll turn on you. Trust me." John scoffed.

"I can offer them love. Crazy as this may seem to you, John, I think that's all they want," Dan said and motioned for John to get back into his car and drive away.

In a fit of rage, John did as directed and sped out of the driveway. Dan went to his car, said something into the radio, and then came back to Amelia, who was standing on the porch with tears in her eyes.

"Did you really mean that?" Amelia asked.

"That jerk." Dan rolled his eyes.

As they stepped into the house, Adam and Meg were standing there. Meg was a ball of raw emotion, crying and wiping her eyes. Adam was struggling to be a man while still having the feelings of a boy. They held each other's hands like they had when they were little.

"You really want to adopt us?" Meg asked.

"Of course I do," Dan said as he took a few steps into the house and let go of Amelia's hand. "But at this point,

"Cam we call you 'Dad' anyway?" Adam asked.

"You can call me anything you like." Dan shrugged. "Just don't call me late to dinner." He tried to smile, but the kids just stared at him.

"That's good you say that because Meg and I decided a while back that we think you look like a Pop." Adam squared his shoulders. Tears flickered in the corners of his eyes but never spilled over.

"'Pop'?" Dan chuckled, his own eyes brimming with tears. "I love it."

Meg dashed into his arms again and hugged him tightly. "Pop, is it okay if I call Katherine and tell her what happened? It sure was exciting. I don't think the shoot-out scene in *Tombstone* was nearly as exciting."

"That's up to your mom," Dan said, kissing his new daughter on the head before she got the nod from Amelia and dashed upstairs to her room and her phone.

Adam walked up, extended his hand, and shook Dan's before being pulled in for the biggest, tightest hug he'd ever felt. He hugged Dan back.

"I'm gonna go call Amy," Adam said proudly.

Amelia walked up behind Dan, slipped her hand in his, and pulled him down toward her.

"I love you," she whispered.

"I love you," he replied.

CHAPTER NINE

THE NEXT DAY, after telling Lila and Beatrice the exciting news, Amelia finally calmed down enough to update them on the truck.

"The paint job will be done next week. Then, Beatrice, I'd like it if you'd give it a test-drive and see how all the gizmos inside work. How are things coming with Lionel Hascolm?"

Beatrice stopped what she was doing, looked off into space, and lifted her chin.

"He's been contacted. I'll expect a reply shortly."

"Well, did he sound interested?" Lila asked.

"I don't know. We've only communicated through text since graduation," Beatrice answered then went back to her baking. The green tea cupcakes with ginger frosting were flying out of the truck faster than Beatrice could bake them. A problem they hoped to solve with another truck and baker.

"Why do you only communicate through text?" Lila asked. "These kids today. They don't know how to sit down and have a conversation."

"That isn't it, Lila," Beatrice said calmly. "In order to woo the raven, one must tread softly. You aren't just hiring some kid to work a fast-food counter. You are not looking to hire just a baker who can throw ingredients together and come up with a halfway decent product. The Pink Cupcake has come too far for that. You need a true artist, and as much as I hate to admit it, I'm more than slightly intimidated by being in this unique position."

"What is that, Bea?" Amelia asked.

"I'd be his supervisor," she replied.

"You would be, Beatrice. Because you are the greatest baker I've ever seen. You've not only stayed true to my plan for The Pink Cupcake, but you've contributed in making it better," Amelia said. "I hope this Lionel fellow is as good as you say. But even if he's a thousand times better, he isn't you. You are part of the original family. And you always will be."

Before Amelia could say anything else, Beatrice had shuffled across the length of the truck from her baking station to Amelia, wrapped her arms tightly around her waist, and squeezed.

"Thank you, Amelia." Then, Lila got the same treatment. "I'm sorry. I don't like to get emotional, but that's the kindest thing anyone has ever said to me." She rubbed her cheeks, transferring more flour to them before going back to work.

"Hello up there? Am I interrupting you gals?"

Amelia and Lila both looked out the service counter window at the same time. Amelia instantly recognized the man. Detective Hobbs.

"Hi, Detective. What a nice surprise," Amelia said. "What can I get for you?"

"I was hoping you might have some of those chocolate cupcakes my Lucy loves so much," he said, casually rocking back and forth on his heels.

"If you can just give me a couple minutes, I can whip a few up for you," Amelia said.

"I don't want to cause too much trouble. It's just I'm in the doghouse. I forgot her birthday and..." Detective Hobbs peeked up from beneath a wrinkled brow, looking just like an English bulldog.

"You forgot her birthday?" Lila asked. "Uh-oh. Amelia, better make those a double."

"I'm on it," Amelia shouted from the back of the truck before sticking a batch in the oven, setting the timer, and then hopping down the steps to join the detective outside.

"They'll be done in just a few minutes, Detective."

"I do appreciate it. That's something you women have always had on us men. You know your way around a kitchen whether you like it or not." He smiled innocently. Amelia chuckled. She wasn't about to argue with him when he was one-hundred-percent right in her case.

"So, has there been any movement on the murder at The Old Barn?" Amelia asked.

She didn't have a gut feeling about anyone and thought if Detective Hobbs had spoken with Rosa and Ronny, maybe she wouldn't have to go snooping around The Old Barn estate.

"I'm going to tell you something, Ms. Harley, and that is murder is an ugly business. You see the worst of people. And you know how I know it's the worst? Because people always try and put on their best faces. I hate to tell them I can see right through it." Detective Hobbs clicked his tongue and shook his head.

"I happened to see Mr. Hope at a restaurant the other night," Amelia confessed.

"Yeah, he was with that blonde." The detective huffed.

"Oh, you were following him?" Amelia asked, hoping she wasn't sounding too eager.

"We always look at the spouse first. Like I said. It's an ugly business," he replied.

Amelia couldn't help but think of John at that moment. As much as she'd grown to dislike him, murder had never crossed her mind. Perhaps a severe butt whipping. But not murder. She couldn't be sure he didn't think the contrary regarding her. Especially after what happened with Dan. But she quickly put the idea out of her head.

"Do you think he did it?" Amelia came right out and asked, thinking Detective Hobbs was a straight-up kind of man, who would know when someone was fishing for information. Better to be blunt and have him shoot her down than play him for a rookie.

"I can't say for sure. The assistant was in the house but then so were the gardener and the maid. Sounds like we're playing a game of Clue, doesn't it?" He smiled.

"Sure does," Amelia replied. Just then, she heard the ping of her oven timer. "I think your cupcakes should be almost ready."

She went up into the truck and, within seconds,

had whipped up the chocolate frosting as she let the small batch of a half dozen chocolate truffle cupcakes cool. After slathering them with the frosting and dusting them with edible silver balls and granulated chocolate sprinkles, she placed them in a bright-pink box and tied them with black string. Then, she placed them in a bright-pink bag with The Pink Cupcake's logo on the side.

"Here you go, Detective. I hope Lucy enjoys them," Amelia said, handing him the bag.

"How much do I owe you, young lady?"

"Of course they are on the house. Cops don't ever pay at The Pink Cupcake." She winked. "Besides, I heard a lot of good things about you."

"From who?" He instantly looked suspicious as if no one should ever be saying good things about him.

"Detective Walishovsky," she replied proudly.

"Wait a minute. You're not the pretty little thing he's been going on and on about over the past year or so, are you? Why, congratulations are in order. He's certainly a lucky man. A woman who can cook and is easy on the eyes is hard to come by," Detective Hobbs said. "Nearly impossible these days."

"Thank you, Detective," Amelia said as more of a question than anything else.

Even though his comments were what some

people might call offensive, Amelia couldn't help but like him. For a man whose job included seeing the worst in people, he was refreshingly pleasant, and she hoped the cupcakes would help smooth things over with Lucy. But more than that, he shared enough information with her that made her decide one last visit to The Old Barn was necessary. She had to meet Rosa and Ronny, the gardener. But how was she going to do it? Samuel Hope knew who she was, and so did Malcolm Wayne. She couldn't just pretend she was there to book the place for her wedding.

But I could be a guest of someone having an event. Like a fundraiser, Amelia thought.

Sondra Hope had said there was a huge fundraiser taking place in four days. That would be tonight. If she just happened to be there, blending in, not drawing any attention to herself, she might crack this wide open. Of course, if Detective Hobbs knew about Samuel Hope and the blonde, he'd probably be watching the place too. She'd have to be extra careful not to attract any attention to herself. Of course, that was always easier said than done.

CHAPTER TEN

WHEN AMELIA SHOWED up at The Old Barn, it was exactly as she'd hoped. Off the driveway, valets took the cars and parked them in a large patch of grass as if they were attending a carnival. Amelia, anticipating making a quick getaway, parked on the street behind a Mercedes and a Tesla, whose drivers obviously had the same idea.

As she looked up at the farmhouse, she saw lots of people on the porch sipping cocktails and chatting while servants in starched white jackets and black pants circulated flutes of champagne and hors d'oeuvres.

With her clutch tucked under her arm and her high heels sinking into the grass, she managed to get to the gravel driveway and carefully make her way to the main area of festivities. The barn itself glowed a warm, golden color from the inside and was sharply contrasted by the cool blue of the evening sky as the sun started to set.

Nervously, Amelia looked around for anyone who might be asking for invitations or checking names off a list, but she didn't see anyone. Most of the male guests were dressed in suits, but she did see a couple of guys in jeans and button-down shirts. Almost every woman was in a dress and showcased quite a bit of jewelry. These people had money, but Amelia proudly thought of the new truck she'd just bought and decided not one of them was better off than she was. Besides, she had Dan and the kids. Who could be luckier?

"Champagne?"

"Who? What?" Amelia jumped, making several people look in her direction.

"Would you like a champagne?" asked the young man holding the silver platter of glasses filled with the bubbly liquid.

"Oh, that would be lovely. Thank you," Amelia said, then raised her glass to the folks still staring at her and took a tiny sip. The last thing she needed was for the bubbles to go to her head. So she opted to carry the glass around, as it made her look more like she belonged.

As she mingled through the attendees, she caught a glimpse of the woman she'd seen run to the oilcan smoker just minutes after Sondra Hope had died. She was only about five feet tall and had wide hips. She looked intensely serious until someone yelled, "Rosa!" She snapped her head to the left. It was Samuel.

Amelia gulped, took a sip of her champagne, and retreated from the hot spot to the porch where Sondra fell dead. Boards and a couple of banisters had been removed either by police or by Samuel due to the bloodstains. There was some sad yellow tape that read CAUTION around a couple of orange cones and was positioned across the hole left by the missing boards. No one seemed to pay too much attention to it, but Amelia felt funny stepping over it to approach the door. There was an old man and woman chatting near the door. Amelia approached them and cleared her throat.

"Excuse me. Is the ladies' room in here?" She pointed inside the house.

The man smiled as he looked her up and down.

"I know there is one in the barn, but I'm sure you

can go inside the house. No one has told us any different," he offered.

"Thanks," Amelia said quickly and stepped inside.

The house smelled of vanilla, and it was decorated like an old farmhouse would be. Except the antiques were not for use but strictly for show. It was like a museum that recreated what a farm might look like after the Great Depression. She walked through a sitting room and saw there was a kitchen off the long hallway to the right where the finger food and drinks were being prepared. But the main course would be cooked in the barn or in the smoker out back.

It was obvious to her now how Samuel could have come in the house but not seen Sondra. If he went down the hallway to the kitchen, he could completely miss her if she was in what looked like a small study that opened to a short hallway, leading to the front door and a staircase winding around to the second floor. The reason Amelia was sure that is where Sondra was is the fact that there was more yellow tape crossing off the study. The hardwood floor was covered by a tarp. Her blood had to have fallen there.

Carefully, Amelia crept across the sitting room,

trying to prevent her heels from clicking on the hard-wood floor. She walked painfully on her tiptoes and looked all over the room.

Why would anyone have stabbed her with gardening shears in the study? They could have waited until she was outside in the barn or even further back on the property. Sondra Hope gave the impression she was very hands-on and that very little went past her unnoticed. Anyone could have requested she check something out on the far end of the grounds and done her in back there. If she had all the lovers Samuel said she did, it could have been pinned on any one of them. But this narrowed it down to the people who were normally in the house.

She peeked into the study and leaned over the yellow tape. It looked like the police had collected everything they wanted and left the room to be straightened up by Samuel or Malcolm. Whoever. The yellow tape was not police issue. It was just to keep nosy guests from snooping around.

With that in mind, Amelia awkwardly stepped over the tape and took a long look around. She walked up to the desk and saw a check ledger, the last entry made the day Sondra died, some bills, advertisements for tools of the trade, linen services, temporary waitstaff, and a few bridal magazines, even the one Amelia had been looking at with Christine before their first visit here.

"Nothing out of the ordinary," Amelia said until she looked closer at the check ledger. Had her eyes not fallen in the exact corner of the ledger, she would have never noticed that three pages of checks were missing. That was a total of twelve checks taken after the date of Sondra's death.

"What do you mean you still can't find it?" came a voice behind her. Amelia panicked and quickly darted behind a panel of long curtains just beyond the desk, next to a huge bookcase. Why she didn't just stumble toward the smaller hallway toward the front door, she didn't know. She was stuck now.

"I've looked everywhere. I can't find it." It was a female voice.

"Then, you aren't looking hard enough," came the male voice she'd initially heard.

"She never told Sam or Malcolm. The sneaky witch. She had so many secrets. This has to be her biggest." The woman huffed.

"Look, Rosa, you were the one in the house the most," the man said. "There has got to be some cubbyhole, some loose floorboard, some place where she would have hid it. If we don't find it, then everything is going to be over. We have to find it."

Amelia swallowed hard and held her breath. Her mouth had gone dry, and her toes were starting to go numb from the pointy tips of her heels. But she didn't dare move.

"You think I don't know that, Ronny?" Rosa scoffed. "It has to be in this room. Unless she went outside the house, but she never got her hands dirty, so I can't imagine she'd want to dig around in the dirt to hide it. That I do know."

"I don't know what you know. But if we don't find out where she put it, our plan is as good as dead," Ronny hissed. "Now I have to get back to the shed and lock up."

"Did you look in the shed?" Rosa asked. "Maybe it's in there? Maybe you are the one who should know every inch of that shack and are sitting on it without even knowing it."

"Look, you're starting to panic. Just calm down. We've got time before Samuel is going to get rid of everything. We might still be able to stop him from getting away with this," Ronny said. "We better get back before we are missed."

Amelia carefully pulled the curtain aside and peeked at the duo before they quickly hurried out of the study. What were they talking about? From the sound of it, they knew something about Samuel that no one else did. And that sounded like a motive. Amelia felt behind her and was sure she felt the latch of a door.

"What is that woman doing?" a male voice said behind her.

"I don't know," a woman replied.

"Is there something going on in the house?" another voice chimed in.

Amelia suddenly realized she was hearing some very distinct voices. Slowly, she turned her head to the right to peek over her shoulder and realized she was in front of a French door that looked out to the garden where several guests were milling around.

"Talk about hiding in plain sight," Amelia muttered. She twisted the handle, felt a snap, and was about to step outside but froze.

"Go get Sam." A man in a gray suit and red tie pointed at Amelia. "I think he should know about this," he told his date. She nodded and hurried in the direction of the barn. Quickly, Amelia pulled the curtain aside and stepped back into the middle of the room. She put her hand to her stomach as she tried to think fast. Her eyes skimmed over the books and knickknacks on the bookshelves. It really was a pretty room.

"Excuse me, miss!" one of the servers called to Amelia. "You can't be in there."

"I'm sorry. I was looking for the bathroom," she lied, smiling.

"The restrooms for guests are in the barn," the servant replied with a suspicious look on her face. She was very thin and tall with her blond hair pulled back from her face in a bun. She stared down her thin nose at Amelia, blatantly not believing her.

"I'm sorry. It was rather an emergency. You know how that can be," Amelia said. "In fact, I think it was something in those little salmon squares you guys were serving. I don't think I better stay." She clutched her stomach and headed toward the short hallway that led to the front door and the staircase upstairs. Her feet were screaming inside her shoes. Each step made her ankles wobble and her knees bend deeper as she tried to make a smooth getaway.

"Wait!" the server called, but Amelia hobbled quickly to the front door, grabbed hold of the crystal knob, and gave it a good yank, startling several guests on the front porch. They all stared as Amelia stepped out, pulling the door shut behind her.

As casually as she could, she tottered across the porch, limped down the steps, until finally giving in to the fact she'd done anything but blend seamlessly into her surroundings. She pulled off one heel and then the other, and sprinted down the sloping front yard, following the gravel drive that led to the street. On tenterhooks, she tiptoed as fast as she could to her car, climbed in, and sped away in a cloud of dust and gravel. The sound of people shouting and laughing at her still echoed in her ears.

"Amelia, that was a pathetic display," she muttered as she looked in the rearview mirror, half-expecting a dozen cars to be following her in pursuit. There were none. She let out a deep breath, and after driving for about half an hour away from the scene of the trespassing, she decided to pull into a Cookie's Hot Dogs and get something to eat.

While sitting barefoot in the parking lot on a picnic bench in her fanciest dress, Amelia ate a chili dog with fries and a Coke. The words that Rosa and Ronny had said stuck with her like a sliver in her thumb. What did they mean that Samuel would get away with what he'd done?

She didn't know. But someone was obviously helping themselves to some of the company checks after Sondra's death. That was probably Samuel. If they'd started the business together, why wouldn't they have access to the checkbook, right? But it was obvious Rosa and Ronny weren't interested in the checkbook. It was right there on the desk, and they didn't pay any attention to it. If that's what they were looking for, then they were completely blind. No, that wasn't it. They were looking for something else, and Amelia was sure whatever it was she could find it if she had some time alone in the place.

"But how are you going to get that?" she asked in between bites. She thought of all the pretty things on the bookshelves in the study. That would be the kind of place Dan would enjoy. A room for himself to review his files or just think, and it could be filled with all of his favorite things. The idea made her smile as she finished her meal, then went back to the counter and ordered enough for the kids.

Before she pulled out of the Cookie's Hot Dogs parking lot, Amelia decided to go back to The Old Barn one more time. But she'd go when no one was around. She certainly couldn't go back now. She had to make a plan and thought having a brownie covered in ice cream with chocolate drizzle and peanuts would be just the thing to boost her snooping senses and inspire her. Instead, it made her too full, and she went home to get a shower, rub her feet, and come up with a plan later.

CHAPTER ELEVEN

"YOU AREN'T GOING to believe who's here," Lila said to Amelia as soon as she arrived at The Pink Cupcake for work the following morning.

"Who?"

"Lionel Hascolm," Lila whispered.

"Where is he?" Amelia asked with wide eyes, completely forgetting about The Old Barn and her experience from the night before.

"He's at the picnic table. The one in the straw hat," Lila said and jerked her chin in the direction of the picnic area. There, with his back to them, was a tall, slender fellow in a straw hat like the ones political constituents wear at conventions.

"Are you sure that's him and not a member of the

Republican caucus?" Amelia asked. Just then, there was a loud clatter from inside The Pink Cupcake.

"I'm sure. Bea has been dropping pans and pots and bumping into things since she told me he was coming to speak to us this morning." Lila shook her head. "She's a nervous wreck in there. I don't understand how a girl as weird as she is is suddenly worried about the opinion of that guy."

"Well, we ought to get this over with for her sake," Amelia said. "Give me one minute to set my stuff down, and we'll see what's all the hubbub."

Amelia went inside the truck and saw Beatrice fussing with two ingredients in her hand that looked almost identical. She was staring at them as if they might explode at any second.

"Beatrice, are you okay?" Amelia asked.

"I don't know what's wrong with me. I'm all thumbs this morning," she squawked.

"Did you know that Lionel was coming today?"

"Yes. He texted me last night. I told him that was acceptable. I hope you don't mind," she said, wiping her cheek with the back of her hand.

"No. I'm glad you did. Did you speak to him this morning?" Amelia continued her questioning as if she were collecting information for some top secret operation that needed to be handled with the utmost discretion and care.

"For a moment," Beatrice said before shaking her head and getting back to the orange and poppy seed cupcakes she was supposed to be making.

Amelia was afraid that today might end up being a plain vanilla with cream cheese frosting day. She'd have to put a notice up, saying the gourmet cupcakes will be back tomorrow once the baker gets her faculties back.

"Okay. Well, you take it easy in here. Remember, they are just cupcakes." Amelia patted Beatrice gently on the shoulder before she left and joined Lila, who had been studying Lionel the entire time.

"You know, he barely moved," Lila whispered. "He sat perfectly still. I don't know what he's doing."

"Maybe he's just enjoying the beautiful view and the day. Could that be it? You're as jumpy as Beatrice is." Amelia chuckled.

"My gosh, you are right about that," Lila said.

"Excuse me, Lionel Hascolm?" Amelia called out.

The man straightened even more in his seat before standing up from the picnic table and turning around. He had round spectacles and was wearing a dapper suit with a vintage tie.

"Amelia Harley, I presume. And you are Lila Bergman. It's a pleasure to meet you." He extended his long arm and slender fingers. Amelia shook his hand, and Lila followed. "I've done a fair bit of research on your establishment. You've been written up by some of the most prominent food critics, and from the looks of things, this has all the makings of a successful business not just here but nationwide. Just what I've been looking for."

"Really." Amelia thought Lionel was honest, direct, and very professional. But something wasn't sitting well with her. "Do you have a résumé that I can look at?"

He looked rather shocked at the request but did reach into the inside pocket of his suit jacket and pulled out an envelope that he handed over to Amelia.

"I'll give you a little bit of my background. I am currently working at the Baumgarten Hotel as their second pastry chef under the tutelage of Pastry Chef Felix Crie, who has been featured on—"

"Oh yes. I've seen him on some cooking shows. He has an interesting reputation," Lila added. "How is it working for him?"

"The experience is noteworthy," Lionel replied. "But I must admit that I don't feel he allows for too many experimental flavors in his kitchen. At least not from what I've seen."

"And you know Beatrice. She would be who you would be answering to," Amelia added.

The glimmer in Lionel's eye dulled for a second and then returned.

"Beatrice was by far the only person I ever saw as any kind of competition. She has a gift. That is for sure. She's lucky to have gotten in on the ground floor of such a prosperous enterprise."

There it was again. The thing Amelia didn't like.

"Okay, Lila, do you have any questions?" Amelia asked, tight-lipped, looking at Lila.

"I don't think so," she said curiously.

"Lionel, thank you for paying us a visit. We do have other applicants we are interviewing. So I'll let you know by Monday of our decision."

She watched his expression and saw that he had obviously never been told no before. Amelia reached out, shook his hand firmly, and walked back to the truck. Once inside, she looked at Beatrice, who was staring into one of the oven windows, the red glow highlighting her cheeks and forehead.

"I'm sorry, Beatrice. But Lionel isn't going to work," Amelia said softly.

Just then, Lila came up the stairs and into the back of the truck.

"You didn't like him," Beatrice said.

"No, I didn't," Amelia said. "I don't care how good a baker he is. I just didn't get a good feeling from him. He gave me the impression that if given the chance he'd steal The Pink Cupcake out from under me, and he came across smart enough to do just that. This is our business. We've made it what it is."

Beatrice was staring at Amelia and Lila with her mouth hanging open. "You seriously are not going to hire him? But he was the best baker in my school. They all said he had a gift."

"That's what he said about you," Amelia replied.

"I don't know if you've made the right decision," Beatrice said, her hands in her lap.

"Oh, I did. We're going to give someone else a shot. I think we need to find someone more like you, Beatrice, who wants to have a job they love and loves the job they have. What do you think?" Amelia smiled.

"Quite frankly, I didn't care for his hat," Lila joked. "Anyone who wears a hat like that shouldn't be trusted around desserts."

Beatrice stood up and was back to her old self.

She returned to her workstation and, almost without looking, gathered her supplies from the shelves and racks nearby to start on the next batch of cupcakes. From the looks of it, she was making something new.

"What have you got there?" Amelia asked as she went to the order window.

"I was thinking of a pistachio mocha with a cherry glaze over the top. It would be just a slight variation on your pistachio cream with orange. It's not groundbreaking, but it might be nice."

"That sounds wonderful. Make enough for me to take home to the samplers," Amelia said. "They love your new ideas. In fact, I don't think there has been one they haven't completely devoured."

The tempo and conversation went back to normal now that the idea of hiring Lionel Hascolm was put to rest. Amelia decided to just place a simple ad as she'd done before Beatrice applied and would hope for lightning to strike twice. Stranger things have happened.

CHAPTER TWELVE

IT HAD BEEN three days since Amelia had tried to seamlessly blend in at the fundraising event that had taken place at The Old Barn, and her toes were finally getting the feeling back in them after being pinched to a point. Her phone had been ringing off the hook with follow-up calls to venues she'd looked into. She'd put a wedding dress on hold that she really liked at the time, but then had second and third thoughts about it by the time she pulled out of the store parking lot. She never called back or stopped in to discuss it further.

What was wrong with her? She couldn't wait to marry Dan. She was crazy about him. But all of this planning and scheduling and decision-making that might have meant something the first time around seemed absolutely ridiculous for her second marriage. Someone even asked Christine if Amelia was having a bridal shower.

"A bridal shower?" Amelia gasped. "Why would I do that? I have everything. Twice. Dan has all his stuff too." But apparently that was now a *thing*. That second marriages, no matter how old the bride was, were worthy of a bridal shower. The world of matrimony had gone crazy, and it was trying to drag Amelia along with it. And then charge her exorbitant amounts of money to do so.

It was one of her greatest pleasures to sit at her kitchen table with a cup of hot coffee, a slice of thick, buttery pound cake that deserved another slathering of butter across the top, and the newspaper. The kids had already gone out to enjoy their Saturday morning with friends. Dan was at his apartment getting some rest for the afternoon shift. Amelia had the house to herself with the only distraction being a cardinal chirping outside and the wind chime Meg had hung by the kitchen window.

As she unfolded the newspaper, she took her time, scanning every page until a small headline on the real estate page made her choke on her coffee.

"Samuel Hope, husband of the late Sondra Hope, owner of The Old Barn Banquets, has announced the sale of The Old Barn. After the untimely death of his wife, Sondra, who was murdered in broad daylight..." Amelia silently read the rest as her mind was reeling. "Mr. Hope will be staying in nearby Will County with family as the property is put up for sale."

It was just the news Amelia needed. Hopefully, Rosa and Ronny hadn't found whatever it was they were looking for. Now the question was, does she go over there now or wait until nightfall? Thankfully, her children made the decision for her. Within minutes of reading the article and taking a few sips of coffee, Amelia got a call from Meg, begging to spend the night at Katherine's house.

"Her family is going to Rockin' Lanes tonight for bowling, and it's so much fun there. Can I stay? Please, please?" Meg asked.

"Now, I was sure I had a list of chores you were supposed to do, and we still have to find you a dress for the wedding," Amelia teased.

"Oh, Mom, no one is going to be paying attention to me. They always just focus on the bride. I could wear a toga and no one would notice," Meg griped.

"You know, that is a great idea. Maybe we should make it a toga wedding." Amelia laughed. "Then, when the ceremony is over, we just put our outfits back on our beds."

"Mom, you are so weird," Meg said, rolling her eyes loud enough for Amelia to hear.

"Okay, have fun and tell Katherine about my toga wedding idea. I bet she'll like it," Amelia said before telling Meg she loved her more and giving three kisses into the phone.

As if he'd overheard Meg's request, Adam called within minutes, asking if he could stay at his friend Tommy's house.

"They invited me to go to the skate park up in Orland. His dad is taking us," Adam said. There wasn't the breathless anticipation that his sister always displayed.

"Hey, Meg thinks we should have a toga wedding. What do you think? Everyone wear a toga?" Amelia asked.

"Okay, but where will you put the vomitorium?" Adam asked seriously.

"Thanks for ruining my joke. Go and have fun."

Amelia sighed before smiling as her son replied, *"Thanks, Mom."*

It would be a long time to wait, but Amelia didn't think going back to The Old Barn in the middle of the day was a good idea. Even if she were a prospective buyer, saying she was just in the neighborhood at ten o'clock, and thought she'd take a look wasn't completely unheard of. Right?

Perhaps her events were going to be strictly at nighttime. She'd want to know what the place looked like. Maybe an eccentric buyer like herself thought it was bad luck to look at property at any other time of day. There was a myriad of reasons she could give for snooping around the property at dusk. So when the time finally came, Amelia was feeling confident that her plan was going to work out. But, as she was driving to The Old Barn, a nervous feeling settled into the pit of her stomach.

"Of course you're nervous. Only a real head case wouldn't be nervous," she muttered to the steering wheel as she found a place to park three blocks away from the property.

The sun was almost completely behind the horizon leaving a pale cape of purple in the sky before the dark night sky took over. There were just a few stars, and the crescent moon didn't provide much light. Amelia was marching down the sidewalk in a pair of dark sweatpants and gym shoes, thinking that this would be a fairly easy endeavor. But, as she neared the gravel road and looked up the hill to the house that stood before The Old Barn, she started to second-guess herself.

None of the cheerful lights that she'd seen just a few evenings ago were on. The house looked completely deserted. The big barn in the back was shut up tight with only a sickly green lamp over the sliding barn door giving off any light. The smoke-house and the garden shed looked like hunchbacked creatures looming in the distance.

Each step Amelia took was like a cymbal crash against the silent backdrop. Even the crickets seemed to be holding their breath as Amelia snuck across the grounds to the house. It dawned on Amelia that she had no idea how she was going to get inside the house. Then, she remembered the scene she made running out of the house through the front door. She was sure the front door wasn't open, but maybe no one had bothered to check the French door in the study.

Carefully, Amelia hugged the aluminum siding of the house and slipped behind a row of rose bushes. She inhaled deeply and held her breath as the bushes were not just beautiful, but they provided a natural deterrent to prowlers. The thorns were long and sharp and snagged her sweatshirt. Finally, when she reached the French doors, she was sweating and had more than a couple of scratches across her hands and a scrape across her neck.

She was sure they'd checked the door and made sure it was locked. Heck, she wasn't even sure that she'd unlocked it. There was a lot going on that day, and there were mysterious things being said, and several strange things on the bookshelves caught Amelia's eye, like all the wedding books and framed pictures of Sondra with various people. None were of her and Samuel, though. Amelia kept remembering a section of books for the way they were so prettily displayed, stacked and leaning with a pretty ceramic bell in the middle of the display.

She stood outside the French door and pressed her ear against the glass. She didn't hear a thing. After wiping her damp hand on her sweatshirt, Amelia took hold of the pretty curled handle and gave it a twist. Click. Click. It opened.

"Well, I'll be," Amelia whispered before stepping inside.

She pulled the curtains aside and peeked into the dark room. Part of her half-expected to see the ghoulish face of Sondra Hope staring at her from the gloom. But there was nothing. A small night-light outside the hallway gave the study enough light that Amelia could step inside and maneuver around fairly easily. But she'd brought her flashlight again. Before snapping on the beam, she closed the thick curtains tightly and tiptoed over to the study door, stepping gingerly over the spot where she was sure Sondra had bled, and closed it too.

The thing that was so important to Rosa and Ronny was in this room. Amelia shined the light around and let out a deep breath. If she had something to hide, where would she hide it? There was no carpet on the floor. She felt along the walls, tapping every couple of spaces for anything that might sound hollow, but the room was as solid as Fort Knox.

After peeking behind every picture hanging on the wall and feeling underneath the desk and behind the grandfather clock, Amelia was starting to think this was more like a needle in a haystack. She had no idea what she was looking for or where Rosa and Ronny had already looked. She walked up to the bookcase and began to study the books on the shelves to collect her thoughts when she heard a car pull up. Quickly, she snapped off her flashlight and peeked out the French door.

Two people got out, who were also carrying flashlights.

"Rosa and Ronny," Amelia muttered.

They must have had the same idea she had. To

tear the place apart while Samuel Hope was staying with relatives. Without wasting a second, she darted out the second door toward the front door as she had the day she snuck in the house during the fundraiser. Only instead of running out the front door and into the yard, she climbed the staircase, perched on the landing, and listened.

The sound of keys jingling in the door came first. Then, Rosa and Ronny came shuffling in without saying anything. But the silence didn't last long.

"Lock that door," Ronny hissed.

"I know," Rosa replied.

"Look, this has already taken longer than it was supposed to. You were supposed to find out where she put the original before you destroyed the other one." Ronny was angry. "The new version had us in it. You were there when she drew it up. You notarized it."

"Yes, but she wasn't happy about it. You act like she did it willingly," Rosa said as they made their way to the study.

"Who closed this door?" Ronny balked.

"What?" Rosa asked, the annoyance obvious in her voice.

"This door was open yesterday."

"Maybe Sam came back and closed it. Maybe he

couldn't stand to see the blood or something and shut it," Rosa replied as she stomped into the study. With a snap, the lights came on.

"Someone has been here," Ronny shouted. "Look!"

Amelia bit her tongue. She was sure she'd forgotten to pull the French door all the way shut when she stepped inside. A nice cool breeze was probably blowing those heavy curtains enough to get Ronny's attention immediately.

Just as Amelia got to her feet and began backing down the hallway in order to slip in some room to hide, she was grabbed around the waist as a heavy hand clamped across her mouth.

"Don't move," the man hissed in her ear as he lifted her off her feet and carried her downstairs to Ronny and Rosa.

CHAPTER THIRTEEN

AMELIA'S HEART was pounding in her chest. She struggled against the man's grip, wildly kicking her legs and scratching at his hands. What had she done? What was she thinking, breaking into someone's house to go snooping around for something that didn't even concern her? What would Dan think? What if he had to go to the coroner to identify her body? What about Meg and Adam? She reached behind her head to grab a hold of her assailant's hair.

"Ouch!" he shouted before tossing her into the study where she fell to the ground.

"What is going on?" Rosa yelled.

"You two didn't even think to check the house before you got started!"

Amelia looked up at the man speaking. It was Malcolm.

"You were here already," Ronny said, smirking. "We didn't think anyone would come in if you were here. Unless you had a girl or something up there. If anything, you should have been watching the house."

"Who is she? One of your girlfriends?" Rosa looked like she wanted to kill Amelia. She stared at her, and for the first time, Amelia got a good look at the late Mrs. Sondra Hope's maid. She was an older lady, who looked like she could be a mom at Meg's school or a nurse at a hospital. Had her black eyes not been piercing into Amelia's she could be anyone or no one depending on what her mood was.

"No. I'm not one of his girlfriends," Amelia said. She was about to get to her feet when Rosa stepped forward, pulling a revolver from her pocket and pointing it at her.

"What are you doing with that?" Ronny barked.

"I told you to bring it, and you didn't. Now we need it. So just say thank you, and let's move on," Rosa growled.

"Stop it. Jeez, if you two weren't brother and sister, I'd swear you were married the way you fight," Malcolm said, shaking his head.

"That's gross, Malcolm," Ronny said. "Can we

focus on the task at hand? Where is this thing? Rosa says that this is the only room it could be in. If you hadn't killed her with my garden tool, she'd have handed it right over to us."

"Why are you talking about this in front of her?" Rosa asked. "How dumb are you both? She can't identify all of us, but now you're telling her why we are here."

"She won't say a word." Malcolm took a step and towered over Amelia. "Say your prayers, Amelia Harley. You've got about ten minutes left to live."

"Oh, the drama." Rosa walked up and cocked the revolver, raising it level to Amelia before Malcolm stepped in the way.

"Are you crazy? You can't kill her in the house. The blood will spray everywhere. Take her outside to the back of the barn. The weather and the bugs will do half the job for us before the cops find her. Besides, she's just some snooping old biddy. They can't even tie her to us."

Rosa winced as if it was physically painful for her to lower the gun. She nodded and put it back in her pocket. Ronny reached down, grabbed Amelia by her sweatshirt, and yanked her to her feet. Her tailbone throbbed, and her left ankle twinged as though she twisted it when she went down. She couldn't be sure. Everything was happening so fast, yet it felt like slow motion, and like she'd been stuck in this room, in this house, for hours.

"You won't get away with this," Amelia said. "I told everyone I know I was coming here. They knew I wanted to sneak into the house. They also know that I saw you at the Wedding Expo. So don't think that if you kill me, you'll get off scot-free. You'll pay for what you do to me as much as you will for what you did to Sondra."

"You don't know anything about it," Malcolm hissed as he stooped to get in Amelia's face. "Do you know what she did? After these two people worked for her for years? She took them out of her will."

"Her will?" Amelia had gotten it in her head that she was looking for something on par with the Hope Diamond or maybe a Mickey Mantle baseball card. Something that was really special. "You committed murder for the money from this place?" It wasn't what she intended to do but Amelia had to chuckle. "I know this place makes good money, but split it up three ways, and I'm not sure you'll be quite ready to retire on a tropical island."

"This isn't her only property. See, that's the thing. She had Rosa and Ronny in her will, and it was for all of her properties. She's got properties all over the country that add up to a little over ten million dollars. Split that three ways and I think we'll all be very happy," Malcolm said through clenched teeth.

"I'm getting tired of her wasting our time," Ronny said.

"Wait, I hear something," Rosa said, her eyes wide and nervous.

Amelia held her breath and listened. It was a car coming up the long driveway. Should she start screaming now or wait? She didn't know what to do.

"We have every right to be here," Rosa said. "We still have the keys, and we are still on the payroll. They can't do anything to us."

"What about her?" Ronny pointed to Amelia.

Before she could do anything, Malcolm grabbed her by the arm and yanked her toward him. "If you make a peep, I'll snap your neck. Now move."

Before she could make any sudden moves, Malcolm yanked open the closet door and pulled her inside with him. He held her tightly around the waist with one arm and his other hand over her mouth.

Amelia peeked to the left then to the right, trying to see anything in the closet that might help her. Reams of paper, stacks of old wedding and travel magazines were standing in plastic organizers, folded tablecloths, and an old sweater that Amelia figured was for those times when Sondra got cold in her office. Or maybe someone left it behind at some event, and she was waiting for them to come back and claim it. But there was nothing of any use to her. No samurai sword. No Louisville Slugger baseball bat. Nothing of use.

"Just calm down," Ronny hissed.

"I am calm. You calm down. Who is it?"

Through the slats in the closet door, Amelia saw Ronny sidle up to the window and delicately pull the curtain aside. He was wearing big clunky work boots and blue jeans. Hardly a night prowler.

"It's the police," he whispered.

"What are they doing here? They shouldn't be here. They finished their investigation. What are they going to do? Take more of the floorboards?" Rosa asked.

"Hit the lights," Ronny said, quickly dashing to the other side of the room.

"What? Shut off the lights for what? That's what guilty people would do. I suppose you want to just hide under the bed upstairs too," Rosa argued.

"Knock knock!"

Amelia's heart jumped as she heard the familiar voice of Detective Hobbs. In a matter of seconds, he was in the doorway of the study, and from the sound of it, he didn't come alone.

"Well, what do we have going on here? Looks like you were right, Samuel. There was a party going on without you."

"Mr. Hope. We were just... we were just here to collect some of our things," Rosa said, smiling pitifully.

"What things would you have left in my wife's office?" Samuel asked.

"Now, leave the questioning to me, Mr. Hope. Did you give any of your employees permission to come on the premises in your absence?" Detective Hobbs asked.

"I did not."

"So as I see it, ma'am, you are trespassing. Now, I know that there are a lot of ladies who think that if they work at a place that entitles them to helping themselves to the petty cash drawer or some very bold women who think they should have access to the boss himself. Wife be damned. Which one are you?" Hobbs asked.

His question made Amelia roll her eyes.

"I'm not either," Rosa started. "Like I said. I was just here because—"

"Look, Mr. Hope didn't take our keys away. He

said we were still to show up for work while the property was being sold."

Amelia squinted through the slats and saw Ronny visibly sweating.

"You often work at this hour? You must be some kind of genius to do the landscaping at this hour in the dark." Hobbs chortled. "You didn't tell me you had a nocturnal gardener, Hope. That could have saved us a trip out here had I known he was just trimming the tulips."

"Ronny, be quiet," Rosa hissed.

"I don't appreciate being accused of this," Ronny said.

"No one's accusing you of anything. Not yet," Hobbs said as he started to chuckle. "I don't know. He's a rather nervous Nellie. I don't know if I'd trust him with my garden tools, Mr. Hope. Ronny, when we spoke, you told me that you worked every day for the past seven years. You had a relationship with the Hopes. You'd never do anything to bite the hand that fed you for so long, now would you?"

Amelia could hear Ronny breathing. He was losing it. He was starting to pant like a cornered dog. She could hear him shuffling his feet. Behind her, she could feel Malcolm's body tightening as Ronny continued to freak out. His grip around her was getting so tight she was finding it hard to breathe. He wasn't leaving her enough space to inhale properly through her nose. If he didn't ease up, she was going to pass out. Then, she realized she had one last option, and, hopefully, it wouldn't result in him snapping her neck.

"Argh!" Ronny charged toward the open study door leading to the front door. Something was there that collided with the man, causing him to fall to the floor with a heavy thud.

Amelia bit down as hard as she could on Malcolm's hand. At first, he clamped down harder on her, squeezing her around the middle, and smooshing her face. But she didn't relent. Instead, she bit harder, and, within seconds, Malcolm was screaming.

"No!" Rosa shouted as Amelia felt Malcolm's grip loosen. Without hesitating, Amelia pushed the door open and fell flat to the floor.

"What the heck is going on here?" Hobbs shouted, his weapon raised along with the other officers', including the one that had stopped Ronny from escaping out the front door.

Amelia didn't move, her eyes wide with her hands over her head.

"Why, Ms. Harley. What in the world are you

doing here? Are you part of this?" Hobbs asked as he reached down, offering her a hand. "I'm going to have to arrest you for breaking and entering. Unless you work here too... at night... like the tree trimmer over there on the floor."

"No sir. I did break in. Well, the door was open." She nodded her head toward the French doors. "But I wasn't invited or allowed to be here." She got to her feet and looked at the bookcase. She spotted her favorite nook before turning to Samuel.

"So why are you here?" Hobbs asked. "And why were you in the closet with Mr. Universe?"

Malcolm was standing there with his hands up in the "I surrender" pose.

"Officer, I can clear this up," Malcolm said while shaking his hand that Amelia had bit down on. "You see, Amelia and I have been having an affair and—"

"Oh, we have not." Amelia laughed. "I'd rather go to jail."

"Yikes, son. You might want to get your story straight before you start speaking for the lady. Some of them might really need a man to tell them what to say, but I don't believe Ms. Harley is one of those women." Hobbs chuckled without smiling.

"Mr. Hope." Amelia cleared her throat. "On the day your wife died, I saw Rosa go to the smokehouse with a stack of papers. She burned something that was obviously important. I came back and sifted through the ashes and only found this tiny bit left." She pulled the paper she'd found from her pocket and handed it to Samuel. "It looks like it's from a will."

"Our will? Rosa, is this true?" Samuel looked at the woman, who defiantly held her head up but said nothing.

"Then I was here again the other night when you had a fundraiser." Amelia sighed. "I thought I might find something if I just had a chance to look around."

"Wait. You weren't the crazy lady running barefoot across the lawn who people were telling me about?" Samuel screwed up his face.

Hobbs remained stoic, and Malcolm shifted nervously from one foot to the other.

"Yeah." She felt her cheeks heat up and was sure they were crazy red with embarrassment. "Anyway, Rosa and Ronny came in here and were saying they needed to find something your late wife had hidden, but they didn't know where."

"You have any idea what she's talking about?" Hobbs asked Samuel, who shook his head before folding his arms.

"I'm sorry. I don't know either," Amelia said and

looked around the room. But it was at the instant that Hobbs said he was going to cuff everyone and take them downtown that Amelia saw what had stuck in her mind for so long. She pointed to the nook with the books and the bell.

"What is it, Ms. Harley?" Hobbs asked.

"Mr. Hope. Your wife and I have the same dictionary." She smiled broadly. "May I?" She pointed and slowly took a couple steps toward the bookshelf, keeping her hands raised.

When she pulled the book down, it was not nearly as heavy as a real dictionary. She flipped the book around and held it up for the detective and Mr. Hope to see. There was a lock on it.

"Well, I'll be damned," Samuel said. "I didn't know she had that."

Rosa looked like she was seeing a ghost. She shook her head, and Amelia could see her jaw working as she clenched her teeth.

"Mr. Hope, would you happen to know where the key would be?" Amelia asked.

"Check in the desk." He shrugged. "Everything that helped her run the business and stay organized was in here. I can't imagine her keeping it somewhere else."

"Hold on, Ms. Harley," Hobbs said, waving her

away from the desk. "Safety first." He went to the desk himself and pulled the top drawer open.

"That's it." Amelia pointed to a little black key in the right-hand corner of the drawer. "It looks just like the one I have."

Detective Hobbs took the key and opened up the box that looked like a dictionary.

"That's just great, Rosa!" Ronny screamed.

"How was I supposed to know?" she screamed back. "Malcolm was the one in her pants. Why don't you ask him why he didn't know about this?"

Malcolm stood still, pale as a ghost, and not able to say a word.

"Now, let's not use profanity about the deceased. Especially coming from a lady," Detective Hobbs said, looking contemptuously at Rosa. "You want us to hold the door open for you, but you talk like that? Good luck. Here, Mr. Hope. Maybe you can make heads or tails out of this."

He handed the box to Samuel, who unfolded what looked like the will.

"This is the will we did together when we first got married." He swallowed hard as his eyes scanned the document before filling with tears. "At the time, she left everything to me. But she said she redid the will. When she told me she was leaving me, she said I'd never get a penny of the place."

"That isn't true. She changed her will," Rosa shouted. "That will is outdated. There isn't supposed to be any more copies. I burned them. I burned them all! It isn't the most current one. Tell them, Malcolm. She left everything to you and the rest of the staff in her new will."

"She didn't make the new will, did she, Malcolm?" Detective Hobbs asked quietly. "That's why you stabbed her with garden shears. It was the first thing you could get your hands on. Ronny had come into the house looking for her to ask about flowers for an event. He'd been trimming the rose bushes outside, and in your fit of rage, you tore them away from him and stabbed her. Then, when you stumbled on the porch after, you realized you had to explain the blood that had gotten on your own clothes, so you held her in your arms and tampered with the evidence, trying to rub off your prints at the same time and get as much of her blood on your clothes as possible."

"She said she loved me," Malcolm blubbered.

"You didn't love her. You loved her money," Amelia said. "And, Detective, there were also some checks missing from her checkbook after the day of

Mrs. Hope's death. You might want to see what was being charged on her credit cards and where checks were being cashed too."

"You told me those checks were safe!" Rosa screamed.

"They were. I mean, I told you to wait to d-deposit them. D-did you w-wait?" Malcolm stuttered. "I told you they were good if you would just wait to deposit them."

"Oh, Miss Rosa, were you cashing checks from the account of the deceased Mrs. Hope? That can be up to seven years for fraud. On top of conspiracy to commit murder, I'd say all of you are looking at a nice long vacation. Except you, Mr. Wayne. First degree murder is as bad as it gets. Hope you like the color orange," Detective Hobbs said as he waved for his officers to cuff everyone.

"What about me?" Amelia asked sheepishly.

"I still don't understand why you were doing all this?" Detective Hobbs asked, scratching his balding head.

"I was here that day to see about The Old Barn for my wedding reception. I felt so awful and thought a woman doesn't just fall on a set of gardening shears. She helped people remember their special day. For all her flaws in her own life, she was helping people celebrate love. I guess that just meant something to me," Amelia said.

"Mr. Hope. I'll let it be your call," Detective Hobbs said as he turned to the big brute, who was crying like a baby.

Amelia and the detective exchanged looks before Samuel spoke.

"My wife left a note in here dated just one month ago. It says she is sorry things didn't work out and that it was nothing I had done. But she said, if anything happened to her, she wanted me to have everything because it was our wedding that made her first believe in love and continue to provide that kind of romance to our guests. Silly, right? I mean, she cheated on me, and we fought. But she didn't completely hate me. Not completely." Samuel sniffled but smiled through his tears. "No. I don't want to press charges against Ms. Harley. If it weren't for her, I would have never found this." He waved the pretty little note on flowery stationery.

Amelia let out a deep breath and smoothed the hair on the nape of her neck. She stepped back as the officers cuffed everyone else and read them their Miranda rights. As she watched everything that was happening, she walked up to Detective Hobbs while he was mumbling and scribbling notes in his pocket notebook.

"Did Lucy like her cupcakes?" she asked.

"Well, let me just say that I didn't have to sleep on the couch. For that, I thank you. I don't think it's so bad for a woman's place to be in the kitchen, especially when she bakes like you. But I'm afraid I'm going to have to tell Dan about this," the detective said.

"That's okay. I hate to say it, but I think he's used to it by now." Amelia smiled and, after getting the green light to leave, walked back to her car and went home.

CHAPTER FOURTEEN

IT HAD BEEN a week after the news of the scandal at The Old Barn hit the papers. Amelia was glad it was over, so that now she could focus on her wedding.

"Just relax," Lila said. "It will all fall into place. They always do. You freak out until the very last minute, then everything just magically comes together."

"Lila, Dan and I agreed to have one of the judges he knows marry us. He could only do it on the eighth of next month, which means the wedding is a month away, and I don't have a dress, a venue, a caterer, or a DJ. What's wrong with me?"

No matter how much she tried to reason with herself, she just couldn't muster up the energy to plan this wedding. It hung over her like Spanish moss and made her feel nervous and suffocated. But every time she was with Dan, he was as cool as a cucumber and able to focus on work while still being relaxed and fun around the kids. What was wrong with him?

"Okay, I've had enough. From this moment on, Amelia Harley, soon-to-be-Walishovsky, I am taking over the reins. You are not to think about the wedding at all. I'll handle it." Lila took out her phone and began to make a few calls.

"Who are you calling?" Amelia asked.

"None of your business. Besides, you've got The Pink Cupcake to worry about. Don't we have a second truck to pick up?" Lila asked.

Beatrice nodded as she made jalapeño pepper cupcakes. They were new and went hand in hand with the chili corn bread cupcakes that people were scarfing down faster than they could make them.

"Oh! Yes, that's today. Right now. I'll be back shortly." Amelia had grabbed her purse and was about to jump from the back of the truck when a tall young man with blue eyes and a bulbous nose nervously asked for the proprietor.

"That would be me," Amelia snapped.

"Hello. My name is Karl Heathers. I'm replying to your ad for a baker."

He was a young man somewhere in his twenties, and although he wasn't what Amelia would call handsome in the traditional sense, he was a striking young man and very personable. The second truck would have to wait.

After taking a seat at the picnic table to talk, Amelia went right for the jugular. "Karl, can you tell me what you like about baking? That's all you'll be doing."

"Well, I hope so. You see, my grandmother taught me how to bake. I didn't go to any school. But I've been baking my whole life and can't think of anything better than to try a few new twists on some old favorites. That seems to be what you do. That's why I thought we'd make a good match." He smiled.

"You sound very much like our current baker. You'd be answering to her, and she did go to a baking school, but I think you might be able to find some common ground," Amelia said firmly.

She liked Karl. But she had to get Lila's opinion before she'd commit to anything. Within minutes, Lila was putting Karl through her own line of questioning, but, by the time she was finished, Karl had said something that tickled her funny bone and made her laugh. That was a good sign.

Finally, it was Beatrice's turn. She washed her hands and straightened her hot pink blouse until the words The Pink Cupcake were smoothed out. It was the strangest sight Amelia and Lila had ever seen, and where Beatrice was concerned, that was saying something.

"Is she... is she flirting with him?" Amelia asked as they watched them sitting at the picnic table together.

"Uh-oh. How do we feel about that kind of behavior between coworkers?" Lila asked.

"They'll be at two separate trucks at two locations. I don't care what they do after-hours. Do you?" Amelia asked Lila.

"Are you kidding? I'll want to know every detail about what those two do after-hours. He looks like a young Karl Malden, doesn't he?" Lila smiled.

"That's who I was thinking of. That's who Beatrice says was her Hollywood heartthrob, remember? We both thought she was a little screwy, but, for Beatrice, it's a perfect fit. She's not like other girls."

"That's for sure." Lila chuckled.

"I think we found our new baker." Amelia smiled.

"I knew once you let go of all this wedding stuff and let me handle it, everything would fall into place." Lila nodded.

"Would you give him the good news for me? I want to get the truck before they close," Amelia said, slinging her purse over her shoulder.

Lila waved her away, then walked over to the picnic table. After a little chitchat, she asked Karl if he'd like to start on Monday. He agreed. And, before he left, Lila saw him give Beatrice a small piece of paper.

"What was that?" Lila asked, teasing.

"Doesn't he look like Karl Malden?" Beatrice tittered.

"Slightly. What did he give you?"

"He learned to cook from his grandmother, who lived with him his whole life. Isn't that sweet? And his favorite spice is allspice. I can hardly wait until Monday." Beatrice swooned.

"What was on that little piece of paper, Beatrice? Tell me now," Lila scolded. "Is it his phone number? Beatrice, hasn't your mother ever told you that a lady never calls a gentleman? He's supposed to call her if he's worth his salt."

"It's not his phone number. It's his recipe for raspberry-peach-and-lemon cake with a lime glaze that he swears tastes like sherbet." Beatrice giggled like she momentarily lost her mind. "I'll make it this weekend." She squealed before going back to her baking station.

Lila smiled and shook her head as she leaned over the service counter to take an order.

Amelia had made it to the detailing shop with fifteen minutes to spare. When she walked in, the owner came to greet her with a look of concern on his face.

"What's the matter, Tony?" Amelia asked. "Something happen to my truck?" She had been regularly doing business with these guys as they did her initial paint job for the original truck but had also done some touch-ups and detailing over the past several months to keep it looking good.

"I'm sorry, Ms. Harley. But we got a new guy on the detailing. He got confused with the font you normally use, and instead of 'The Pink Cupcake' being in the usual Apple Chancery font, he did it in Edwardian Script."

Amelia took a look at it, and her heart skipped a

beat. It was a beautiful, elegant, and swirly script that made the truck look a little fancier. But she wasn't going to let on she was okay with the mistake.

"Tony, I'm opening Monday. I don't have time to have it redone. How can you make this right?" She played like she was desperate.

"I'll charge just for the paint. Wipe the labor for the script off the bill. Will that work?" Tony pouted his thick lips and looked at her with puppy dog eyes.

"That will work nicely. Thank you, Tony."

That was almost three hundred dollars off the bill. Amelia was ecstatic. She couldn't have asked for a more accommodating mistake.

When she got home that evening, the kids were doing their homework in their rooms, and Dan had called to say he'd be stopping by around nine for a quick nap and then back to the station. There was a cold case he was helping heat up, and they were closing in on a suspect.

Amelia didn't think about the wedding at all. She watched some television, caught up on some publicity on the internet, and printed a couple more reviews of The Pink Cupcake.

So when the doorbell rang at seven, Amelia was surprised. But not as surprised as she was when she opened the door.

"Hi, Amelia." It was Jennifer, John's wife. She was a beautiful girl, there was no denying that. And she didn't look like she'd had a baby just a short while ago. Amelia stood with her arm across the door and studied the woman. Jennifer looked like she was ready to fight if she had to but was hoping beneath it all that it wouldn't come to that. Amelia hadn't ever been formally introduced but had seen her on several occasions in the car when John dropped the kids off.

"Jennifer. Hello. What... are you doing here?" Amelia knew her voice sounded cold and sharp, but the girl did knowingly sleep with her husband.

"I just wanted to stop by and give you this." She handed Amelia a pretty box wrapped in silver and gold wedding-themed wrapping paper. "John had mentioned you were getting married. Congratulations."

"Thank you?" Amelia asked more than said.

"You're welcome. Well, that was all I wanted to say." She started to back up, and Amelia started to shut the door when Jennifer stopped. "One more thing. I'm divorcing John."

Amelia's mouth fell open, and she just stared.

"He's cheating on me. Can you believe that?" Jennifer huffed.

"Quite frankly, yes I can." Amelia didn't mean to

say it. The words just sort of jumped from her brain, off her tongue, and out into the world.

"Sure. Well, congratulations, again," Jennifer said before walking away.

Amelia opened the box to see the gift: a fancy wine decanter.

She couldn't wait for Dan to arrive. What a day she had to tell him about.

CHAPTER FIFTEEN

THE DAY HAD BEEN cloudy with sprinkles of rain falling throughout. Amelia stood in her kitchen, wearing a pink dress that made her look like she stepped out of a 1950s vintage magazine. She wore pink pumps that Meg had picked out that were the same color as The Pink Cupcake and matched the little gloves her daughter insisted she wear and the pillbox hat.

"Mom, you look amazing. I want to get married in a dress just like that," Meg said.

"Well, anything you want, honey, and we'll do it," Amelia said.

"I just saw Dan pull up. The judge is with him and so is Detective Hobbs, if you can believe it." Lila smiled as she sauntered into the house.

"Oh, Lila. I would have been so lost without you. I can't believe you pulled this off in no time, and here I was, spinning my wheels like a crazy person." She walked over to her friend and slipped her arm around her waist. Although Amelia had asked Meg to be her maid of honor, she insisted that Lila be in the bridal party.

"That's what the bridesmaids are for." She squeezed Amelia back. "Now, I'm going to direct that handsome fiancé where to stand. Your son has got some beautiful music playing. When you hear the 'Here Comes the Bride' theme, just come on out."

"I hope it doesn't rain," Meg chirped.

"Are you kidding? Rain is a sign of good luck and a happy marriage," Lila said, winking at Amelia before she went outside.

"Is that true, Mom?"

"That's what they say," Amelia replied as she stood back from the patio door of her home and saw the small gathering of people she cared about in her small backyard. This was better than The Old Barn or any other venue she could have picked. She loved her dress and thought she, Meg, and Lila looked wonderful all in pink.

Under a canopy, she saw Rusty from The

Twisted Spoke restaurant, watching Lila as she walked back and forth like a bulldog staring at a piece of ham. If there was a pair that should get together for good, it was those two. He had trays of pulled pork, miniburgers, sweet potato fries, coleslaw, and potato salad. And next to him were the pink and white cupcakes that Beatrice and Karl had made special for the event. They were also seated outside, waiting for things to get started.

Adam was under a canopy with his computer and iPod or whatever it was that he'd programmed all the music into. They collected everyone's favorite songs and promised to play them all well into the night if necessary. Christine had requested at least a dozen songs she wanted to dance to and was there with her husband and four boys, who were doing their best to sit still and behave.

Amelia was surprised at how calm and relaxed she was. She smoothed out the front of her dress and thought about how it was just a short while ago that she'd moved into this house, afraid, lonely, and hurt because she had been dumped by the man she thought she loved. Looking back, John had a lot of issues that she only saw after meeting Dan and catching a glimpse of what true happiness could be.

Amelia heard her cue.

"Mom! Are you ready?" Meg asked, followed by Lila, who hurried inside to give Amelia's dress one last fluff and pat.

"I'm ready," Amelia said, and before she knew it, she was outside.

Lila and her daughter walked down the little grass aisle between the sets of chairs, and Adam was at her side.

"You look real pretty, Mom."

"Thanks, honey."

"I thought for sure you'd be crying," Adam said.

"I haven't felt like crying at all. I guess I'm just more in control this time," Amelia said.

"If you say so."

He offered her his arm, and they walked together to the edge of the lawn. Amelia looked up and saw Dan wearing the most handsome black suit with a bright-pink tie. He barely smirked and looked more handsome than ever because Amelia saw tears in his eyes. She couldn't help it. She started to cry too. It was the only way she could express how happy she was.

As she watched Adam shake Dan's hand, her heart pounded with pride. Dan took her hand and held it tightly. He wasn't shaking or nervous, and when he looked down at her, he winked.

"You look beautiful," he whispered.

"So do you," Amelia replied.

"What are you crying about?" he asked, blinking his own bright-blue eyes.

"Because I love you so much. Why are you crying?"

"Same," he replied.

And the judge began. "Dearly beloved, we are gathered here today to celebrate Amelia and Dan..."

RECIPE 1: CORN BREAD CUPCAKES WITH MAPLE BACON

Makes 12

Ingredients:

- 1 1/4 cup flour
- 1/2 cup yellow cornmeal
- 2 teaspoons baking powder
- 1 teaspoon salt
- 1 cup sugar
- 2 tablespoons dark brown sugar
- 2 tablespoons maple syrup
- 1/2 cup buttermilk
- 2 large eggs
- 7 tablespoons unsalted butter, melted and cooled
- 1/4 cup bacon, cooked, drained, and crumbled

Frosting:

- 8 tablespoons butter, room temperature
- 2 1/2 to 3 cups of powdered sugar
- 2 tablespoon maple syrup
- 1 teaspoon maple flavoring
- 2-3 tablespoons half and half
- 3 tablespoons cooked, crisp bacon, crumbled

Preheat oven to 375°F. Prepare cupcake pans with liners. In one bowl, combine flour, cornmeal, baking powder, salt, and both sugars. In another bowl, beat together buttermilk, eggs, syrup, and melted butter. Whisk wet ingredients into dry. Fold in crumbled bacon.

Fill each cupcake liner around 2/3 full. Bake for 20-25 minutes.

Meanwhile, make frosting by creaming butter. Blend powdered sugar in on slow speed. Add maple syrup and flavoring and blend thoroughly. Optional: add milk as needed for icing consistency.

Frost tops of cooled cupcakes. Garnish with cooked bacon.

RECIPE 2: JALAPEÑO CUPCAKES WITH CREAM CHEESE FROSTING

Makes 12

Ingredients:

- 1 1/4 cups all-purpose flour
- 1 cup sugar
- 1/2 cup cornmeal
- 2 teaspoons baking powder
- 1/4 teaspoon salt
- 2 large eggs
- 1/2 cup 2% milk
- 1/2 cup olive oil
- 1/2 teaspoon vanilla extract
- 3/4 cup frozen corn, thawed
- 2 tablespoons seeded jalapeño pepper, finely chopped

FROSTING:

- 4 ounces cream cheese, softened
- 1/4 cup butter, softened
- 1 3/4 cups powdered sugar
- 1 teaspoon vanilla extract
- Sliced jalapeño peppers

Note: Take precautions when cutting hot peppers; the oils can burn skin. Avoid touching your face.

Preheat oven to 400°F. Prepare cupcake pans with liners. In a large bowl, combine the flour, sugar, cornmeal, baking powder, and salt. In another bowl, combine the eggs, milk, oil, and vanilla. Combine wet ingredients into dry ingredients. Fold in corn and jalapeño.

Fill each cupcake liner around 1/2 full. Bake for 20-25 minutes.

In a large bowl, beat cream cheese and butter until fluffy. Add powdered sugar and vanilla; beat until smooth. Frost cooled cupcakes. Garnish with jalapeño slices. Store in the refrigerator.

ABOUT THE AUTHOR

Harper Lin is a *USA TODAY* bestselling cozy mystery author.

When she's not reading or writing mysteries, she loves going to yoga classes, hiking, and hanging out with her family and friends.

For a complete list of her books by series, see her website.

www.HarperLin.com